For Annette —
Many thanks!
AE

THE BATHTUB FULL OF HOLES

Arielle N Eicher

ARIELLE N. EICHER

Josh 24:15

Deep River BOOKS

The Bathtub Full of Holes

Published by Deep River Books
Sisters, Oregon
www.deepriverbooks.com

ISBN – 13: 9781632695918
Library of Congress Control Number: 2022922724

Printed in the USA

Cover design by Jason Enterline
Cover art by Hannah L. Neasham

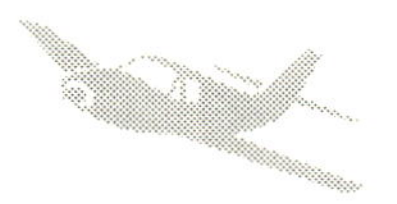

ACKNOWLEDGMENTS

A first book is an adventure. Thanks to all who have helped me along on this ride.

My proofreaders: Janet, Sarah, Hannah, and Abigail Neasham, Patty Small, Dennis and Gloria Dickinson, Daniel and Brittany Eicher.

Mike—I am indebted to you for your technical expertise regarding airplanes, and if I remember correctly, you planted the seed that would grow into the plot of this story.

David—thanks for being my sounding board. I left "Shoes" in just for you.

Thank you, Bill Ziegenbein, for your encouragement. You said I should write books. Here's number one.

A big thank you to Andrew Carmichael and the Deep River Books team for taking a chance on a newbie, and not (quite) telling me to jump in a lake! Nancie Carmichael answered a whole slew of questions. Carolyn Currey made the editing process mostly painless! Thanks also to Tamara Barnet for keeping me on track.

Thanks to Jason Enterline, my cover designer, for searching out that perfect plane and working to get things just right!

Hannah, thank you for adding your personal touch to my cover. I am honored to have a Hannah Original!

To my young fan club: Tirzah, Naomi, Azariah, Reuben, and Keziah Eicher. Many thanks for your enthusiasm in this process and your patience as your Aunt Arie used you as guinea pigs for an unedited manuscript.

To God, who gives all things, both now and in the life to come, to Him alone be glory.

To Mom,
for believing in this book even
when I did not

Follow Arielle N. Eicher
www.arielleneicher.com

TABLE OF CONTENTS

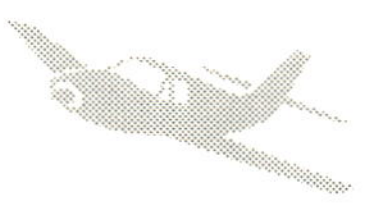

PROLOGUE

The smuggler's eyes never wavered from the white cloth envelope. He swallowed and licked his lips.

"Everything must be ready," said the other man, crushing the envelope in his fist, a clear threat of what would happen if things did not meet with his approval.

The smuggler narrowed his eyes at the childish gesture. It was not as though he had no experience in these matters. "Yes, yes, yes." He waved a hand and paused to straighten the sleeve of his robe. "And then the second half of our transaction . . ."

The other man concealed a growl as a cough. He twisted the ring on his finger and the red gemstone made a full circuit. "Left in a tin of birdseed," he snarled.

The smuggler laughed, a gurgling chuckle, and the other man instinctively cleared his throat.

"In a tin of birdseed," the smuggler repeated. He held out his hand, fingers tingling for the weight of the little white envelope. "Thank you." He stuffed it into his left-hand pocket. "My man will show you out."

CHAPTER ONE

A HYPOTHETICAL PROBLEM

October 1947

A man of exceedingly large proportions, Milford Smith sat at the breakfast table, pencil poised above an old calligraphy tablet. With the other hand, he raised a glass of grapefruit juice to his mouth, slurped, and blotted his lips on the sleeve of his green, quilted robe. He muttered quietly to himself about the figures before him, then the pencil went to scratching again.

A door opened quietly, and Milford's breakfast made its appearance on a large mahogany tray brought on the arms of a butler who was quite as skinny as Milford was not. Ice tinkled musically in the juice pitcher and Milford handed his glass to the man and continued to write:

Total volume—Rate of flow x Time = Z

He stopped and stared at the tablet for a moment, then scratched it out again and threw down his pencil.

"Our little experiment worked rather well, didn't it, Orville?"

"Indeed it did, sir."

Milford smiled. "However, it seems the calculation will prove more difficult than I had at first anticipated. For one thing," Milford paused to bite into a bagel. "Elevation: what works here would not be the same at ten thousand feet above sea level."

Orville considered this a moment. "No, you're right, of course." He shrugged. "Of all your experiments, sir, this one seems most odd! Bathtubs and holes!"

"You think so?" Milford smiled broadly, showing a dental gap at one corner of his mouth. "I thought it a stroke of genius, myself."

"I'm not sure what a genius would be doing bathing in a leaky bathtub, sir. But it could be that I just don't understand, being an average man myself."

"It could be that," Milford allowed.

"At any rate, sir, I think it's a fine thing you're doing now: the study of science is a noble endeavor, and what I said was meant only as an observation."

"But a very good observation," Milford said with a smile that scrunched his eyes up tight. "A good observation from a good man."

"Thank you, sir!" Orville beamed.

"But . . ." Milford added, looking around the table.

"Yes, sir?" A wrinkle creased Orville's brow beneath an ever-thinning, grey comb-over.

Milford pointed across the table and then indicated his eggs. "Sodium chloride, if you please."

"Ah!" said Orville. He passed his employer the salt, and nothing further was said about bathtubs and holes.

ꕥ ꕥ ꕥ

A jumble of his wife's high heels tumbled off the top closet shelf and onto Edward Martin's head. He tugged once more on the handle of his suitcase and ducked beneath its umbrella as the hail persisted.

"Maria! Why are your shoes up here?"

She poked her head out from a mass of her dresses. "There wasn't room on the shoe shelf: you put them up there yourself, darling."

"I put them on the floor, too," he quipped, rubbing his head.

"How many good white shirts do you want?"

"Two or three ought to do it."

"Here are two—oh, but this one is stained."

"Won't matter much if I'm in my suit coat," Eddy commented, laying his suitcase open on the bed. He stopped and stared at his wife. Framed in the closet doorway, she made a very pretty picture: deep green eyes above a retroussé nose, her petite figure set off to advantage in a peaches-and-cream floral. Her new hairstyle wasn't bad, either.

"What? What are you looking at?"

"Oh, just the prettiest thing in all the world," he said lightly.

She turned back to the closet in search of more shirts. "Flattery will get you nowhere. You say I'm pretty one moment and desert me while you fly off to California the next!"

"Maria, I build airplanes: you should expect me to fly occasionally!"

Maria turned back to him with one more shirt in hand. "But Eddy," she pouted, "Mr. Jensen promised you wouldn't be going on these trips anymore!"

"He'd be going himself except for that nasty stomach bug. His wife said she's not letting him out of the house for a week. This deal's big: he asked me to go along and see to it."

"Well, I still hate to think of you flying. Ever since Brad—"

She choked up. It was too recent—not yet six months since she had watched her older brother ride a plane down nose first. Eddy took the shirt from her, threw it into the suitcase, and pulled her close.

"It's okay, Maria. We're not doing circus tricks like Brad. No loops or rolls: just a simple trip to California. And back again."

She nodded and straightened his collar. "I know. Be safe, Eddy."

"Always. For you." He nodded toward the closet. "Did you hide my suit back in the depths?"

"You told me you wouldn't need it again," Maria reminded him, wiping one eye.

"Ah yes. Back into the closet, then. Shall I tie a rope around your waist in case you can't find your way out?"

Maria slapped his arm playfully and dove back into the closet, out again a moment later.

"Madame, you are a marvel!" Edward said. He bent and kissed her hand, then turned it to look at the watch on her wrist. "Fifteen minutes."

"Oh, Eddy! Why do you have to go? He promised!"

"It can't be helped. Look, honey, I design those aircraft; you don't have to worry. Why, flying in one of them is as safe as . . . as safe as soaking in my own bathtub!"

"People have drowned in their own bathtubs before."

"Please, Maria! Is there anything I can say to make you feel better?"

"Sure. Two words."

Eddy kissed his wife on the forehead. "Love you?"

"Uh-uh. 'I'll stay.'"

"I'm sorry, Maria, I—" He stopped and checked the time again. "Ten minutes. Come on, Maria, pack your things!"

"What? Am I going?"

"Sure! Why not? If the boss can take his secretary, why can't I take my wife?" He pulled her suitcase down amid another hail of shoes. "Just get a few things, quick as you can: I'll buy you whatever else you need when we reach LA!"

ꟿ ꟿ ꟿ

Gleaming blue and white, two Beechcraft Bonanzas sat wing to wing on the tarmac, waiting patiently as their mechanic, Benny Ferguson, completed his engine check and replaced the cowling.

"There y'are, girls," he said, pulling a grease rag from his back coverall pocket. "All ready t'go. Yup, all ready t'go." He chuckled to himself and wiped a grimy finger under his nose, leaving a long black smudge.

A cherry-red Rolls Royce Phantom pulled up alongside the hangar, squealing to a stop.

"Hiya Ferggy! How's it going?" A tall, clean-shaven youth hopped out and grabbed a leather duffel with the initials WJW from the back seat. "You got everything in working order? Last time I flew 61Tango, I was getting a bit of a shudder."

Ferguson shrugged. "Check her yourself!" He tossed the grease rag at him.

The young man scowled as the mechanic retreated to the hangar. "Fine help. Check it yourself!" He dropped the rag. A quick pre-flight check of 61Tango found everything satisfactory. But upon taxiing to the fuel station, she hiccuped just a little. It wasn't much. But it was too much. He wanted to fly, not to be bothered with minor mechanics. He taxied back and climbed out to find Ferguson.

But he stopped halfway to the hangar. He was scheduled to fly 61Tango to Los Angeles that afternoon; his passengers would be arriving any minute. Why not take her twin sister, 71Tango, and save some trouble?

He completed a pre-flight on 71Tango, and had her fueled and ready for flight when a cab stopped in. Two guys and a girl climbed out, gathered their luggage, and approached the plane.

"Hello!" called the first man. "I am Jack SuLong," he said, extending his hand. "And these are my friends, Camille Jensen and Carl Linder. We're with Jensen Aircraft Manufacturing."

"Walter Westman," said the pilot with a quick nod. "Is this all of you?"

"We have one more—if he makes it in time. Last-minute changes, you see."

"I've had a few of those myself," Westman admitted. He glanced over his passengers. Jack was short and dark, Asian or Pacific Islander, with the beginnings of a belly, but still very snazzy in a dark-blue, pin-striped business suit with matching blue tie. A fresh gardenia bloomed in his buttonhole.

Carl provided a contrast: dressed casually in tan slacks and a light-knit sweater-vest. His build was thin and wiry, his hair a shock of insubordinate, sandy growth that looked as if he had given up all hopes of taming it. An ingrown smile tugged at the corner of his lips as he squinted up at the sky, anticipating a clear flight.

Camille was pretty enough in feature, and her manner of dress spoke of a cautious experimentation with the lighter colors, the fuller cuts of post war-rationing days. But her step was wooden, with one foot and ankle bound in a brace. A big green bandanna tied around her head and a pair of dark glasses gave the impression of invisibility. The pilot did not bother with a second look.

Westman had only just completed these observations when another car screeched to a halt near his, and a man and woman bailed out. The man grabbed a suitcase in each hand and they ran toward the plane as fast as she could in her heels.

Westman nodded at the pair. "Who is *that?*"

"That is *Mrs.* Edward Martin," said Carl. "And you had better not forget it: I once saw Eddy land a marine sergeant in the hospital for three weeks 'cause he forgot. As I recall, it took several sailors and a couple army guys to haul him off of the fella!"

Westman glared at Carl and grunted in a way that was supposed to mean he was not afraid of a fight. Though in truth, Eddy did not look the sort that you would want to take on just for fun: his friendly demeanor was accompanied by a stout physique—average height, average weight, but sturdy as a brick wall.

"Hey Martin!" Jack called. "You made it!"

"Yeah, I made it. Here, take these, would ya?" He handed Carl both suitcases and sprinted back to the car.

Carl hefted Maria's nearly empty suitcase. "Hey! I think you forgot your toothbrush!"

Eddy was not long in returning with an olive drab, army-issue shoulder bag and canteen.

"Still carrying your kit, eh?" Carl ribbed him, and stowed the last of the bags in the luggage compartment. "You know the surrender was signed two years ago, buddy."

Eddy shrugged and nodded sheepishly. "Never feel quite dressed without it," he admitted.

"All right, enough chitchat, boys," said Jack. "Cub Scout Martin, you're up first."

"Right-o," said Eddy. He handed Maria up into the airplane. She stepped in lightly, running her hand along the polished trim.

"I haven't flown since before the war," she told Eddy. "Remember the first time you took me?"

"You mean the time I showed up instead of your brother? How could I forget? You threatened to box my ears off!"

Maria laughed at the memory. "I used to fly with Brad all the time. That is, when he didn't have someone he liked better. I got to be pretty handy behind the yoke myself."

Eddy smiled. This trip would undoubtedly be good for Maria.

Camille stepped in and sank to her seat, one hand pressed to her forehead.

"Are you all right?" Eddy asked, leaning forward.

Carl hopped up beside her. "You okay?"

"Yes, I'm fine," Camille assured them. "Just moved too fast, is all."

"You and your dizzy spells," said Carl. He patted her hand encouragingly. "Sit tight, kid. You'll feel better in a bit."

Walter settled into the pilot's seat and put on his headset. In the co-pilot's position, Jack lifted his lapel, his nose brushing the gardenia's petals.

Ten years, Jack thought. *Ten long years. No,* he amended with a slight shake of his head. *Six long years. Four short. Incredibly short.*

Westman frowned at Jack. "Where are you going: to meet with a client? Or to a wedding?"

Jack snapped back into the present. "To California," he answered gruffly. "Contact."

The young pilot rolled his eyes and started the engine.

ഗ ര ഗ

Ferguson sat on his three-legged stool, lunch box open in his lap. Pastrami on rye was one of his favorites. And rounded out with pearl onions, deviled eggs, and dill pickles, it was a meal fit for a king. With one exception. He opened the sandwich and peeled a leaf of limp greenery from the bread. Lettuce. It did not matter how often or how vehemently he objected to the slimy weed: it still inevitably found its way into his sandwich. And so, the pre-lunch ritual: he passed the lettuce to the bill of a large green parrot perched atop its cage. The bird took the lettuce in its beak and bobbed up and down happily.

"Pastrami on rye!" it squawked around the leaf.

"Don't talk with your mouth full, Oscar," Ferguson addressed the bird. He took a bite of sandwich, then of pickle. "It ain't polite."

Oscar complied with his suggestion and munched the rest of the lettuce before shrieking again: "What goes up must come down!"

"You're right there, Oscar," Ferguson nodded. "What goes up must come down. But it's my job t' see that it don't come down afore its time!" He chuckled and offered the bird a piece of bread crust. Oscar squawked and took the crumb carefully from Ferguson's fingers.

"Yup, it's my job t' see—" The mechanic paused midsentence, cocking his head to listen as an aircraft buzzed over the hangar. Something was not right. He hurried to the tarmac and stopped in front of the lone Beechcraft. His pastrami on rye hit the pavement.

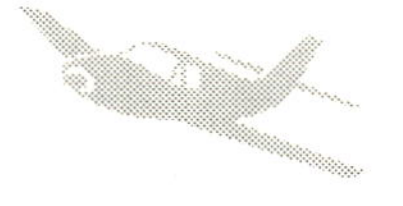

CHAPTER TWO

WHAT GOES UP MUST COME DOWN

Milford did not believe in allowing anything to spoil his breakfast. Nor his lunch. Nor dinner, for that matter. He had shoved aside the puzzling bathtub full of holes in order to enjoy his eggs, bacon, bagels, fresh strawberries, and grapefruit juice. By nine o'clock, however, the calligraphy tablet had once again attracted his attention. He set to work with dogged determination, and two, five, and then seven pages were filled up with formulas, charts, and sketches. The work still went on when, at eleven thirty, Orville informed him that lunch could be served at his convenience.

"Bring it right up," he said with a careless wave of his hand, and continued scratching hasty figures on the tablet. He was eating his lunch, somewhat distracted, when Orville announced he had a visitor waiting to see him.

"Tell him I'm busy," Milford growled. "Tell him I've crawled off and died!" Then, thinking on it a second more, asked, "Well, who is it that intrudes on a poor man's lunch hour like this?"

"It's that policeman, sir."

"Ah, Rigby. No manners. Very well. Better bring a plate for him."

Not two minutes later the inspector appeared on Orville's heels with his usual salutation. "Well, Smith? What have you been up to these days?"

"Up to?" Milford's voice took on an injured tone, and he glared at Rigby over a fried drumstick. "What do you mean by that?"

"You know good and well what I mean, Mr. Smith, and don't you deny it. You're always up to something. Now what is it?"

"Care for some chicken?"

"No, thank you," said the inspector, pulling back a chair. "Perhaps you had better think of this as just a social call, Smith. Just your old friend Rigby come to visit, huh?"

"Huh! Come to visit, have you?" asked Milford, chomping noisily. "Then I think you'd better have some chicken."

"No thanks," said Rigby, popping a strawberry in his mouth. "So what have you been doing, ol' pal?"

"Nothing much. Just the usual."

"The usual, eh? More arms deals with the commies? Or just a minor shipment of black-market goods from south of the border?"

"No," Milford answered with a smile. "The usual: breakfast at eight, lunch at eleven thirty, dinner at six, and bed by nine. Have some chicken, Inspector."

Rigby pushed his fedora back from his forehead. "No thanks," he said, and helped himself to a warm biscuit with butter and jam. Spying the calligraphy tablet on the table, he gestured with his butter knife. "What's this? Taking up calligraphy?"

"I despise calligraphy," Milford answered bluntly. "Worthless loops and twirls. No, Inspector. You'll be glad to know that I'm a retired man now. Naturally, a man who has led an exciting and active life does not want to retire into sedentary uselessness. So I've taken to science—the improvement of the mind through study and observation. My man, Orville, has joined me in this pursuit. You'd be surprised what there is to learn, Inspector, if one only took the time. This new puzzle, for instance: a mathematical calculation concerning our latest experiment. So far it has me stumped, but I intend to take mastery."

The inspector blinked at Milford for several seconds.

"Well, don't look at me as if I had three heads, man! Read it; see for yourself." Milford slid the notebook to Rigby. The inspector flipped through all the pages first, then turned it over and flipped through again; watching for writing on the back sides of the pages. Surprised to find nothing out of place, he turned again to the start of the book and studied Milford's figures, mumbling to himself as he read.

"What? Bathtub full of holes. What kind of cockeyed science is this?" He looked up at Milford and raised one eyebrow. "You're off your rocker, Smith!"

Milford shrugged. "Think what you like. But I have told you already: it is merely a scientific problem that caught my fancy. I have an inquisitive mind, Inspector. Surely you can understand that. Besides, mathematics has always been an area of great interest for me."

"Sure! I know all about that: how many additional runs can I make before the law gets wise to it? What are the odds of being caught red-handed if I deal through so-and-so? Sure! I know all about your brand of mathematics: you always *multiply* my trouble!" Rigby got up to pace. "But this one's new to me. Bathtubs full of holes!" He stopped and leaned across the table toward Milford. "You've been quiet so long, Milford. I was beginning to worry. So now that I've come all the way up here, why don't you just tell me what's cooking?"

"Chicken," Milford responded. "But it's getting cold. You'd better come have some, old boy."

"I don't want any chicken!" Rigby exploded, banging a fist on the table. He sat down and thumped a heaping spoonful of mashed potatoes onto a plate. "Do you have any gravy?"

"Certainly." Milford passed the gravy, leaving greasy smudges on the sterling silver boat.

"Mmm. That's good!" Rigby nodded with his mouth full. "Mighty good. No one cooks like Orville!"

"No, you're right there," agreed Milford. "No one cooks like Orville. Have some chicken?"

"Well, I don't mind if I do," the inspector conceded.

ꕤ ꕤ ꕤ

Ferguson cranked up the radio furiously and took the microphone. "Bonanza 71Tango, Ferguson. Bonanza 71Tango: get down now! You hear me? Get down!"

The radio lay silent for a few seconds, then Westman's voice came over. "Sure, I hear ya, Ferggy. Loud and clear. And I'll come down as soon as I'm good and ready. Meet me in LA and we can talk it over then."

Ferguson gritted his teeth. "That plane ain't going to LA, Westman. You get it down now!"

"It's not, huh? Just step outside and watch it, Ferggy! Over and out."

"No, kid! Get down!"

In the background, Ferguson heard Oscar's sing-song chant: "What goes up must come down! What goes up must come down!"

The mechanic turned a glaring eye on the parrot. "Shut up, stupid bird! Don't you know they're all killed?" He rushed from the hangar and caught a final glimpse of the Bonanza Beechcraft as it turned west and disappeared into the blue.

ꕤ ꕤ ꕤ

It had been a long day already. A long week, in fact. Nothing but run, run, run: everything must be ready to go by Friday! Now here it was Friday, and still he was running. Running to work, then back home again. Running to pack and running to catch the plane. At last he had a breather and it felt good!

Eddy felt his head begin to nod and caught it with a jolt. He looked sideways at Maria to see if he'd disturbed her: she had tired of watching the scenery and was reposed against his shoulder, asleep. She had done her fair share of running, too, he remembered with a smile.

His eyelids were beginning to droop again when Carl looked back, a mischievous expression on his face. He pulled an envelope from his shirt pocket and scribbled a quick note in a strange conglomeration of letters, numbers, and funny little figures that would take a code specialist or a friend to decipher. Eddy quickly understood its meaning: "Did you hear the big to-do between the pilot and mechanic?"

Eddy held up the end of his headset cord. He had never plugged it in; it was providing sound cancellation only.

"Sounded like the mech didn't want us in this plane. Curious, eh?"

Eddy took the paper and wrote a few lines: "It's the custom Bon that Beckett wanted; engine sounds fine: all I need to know."

"And the pilot?" Carl insisted.

Eddy shrugged one shoulder, so as not to disturb Maria. "Low hours . . . but anyone can fly a Bon."

Carl conceded the point with a grin and Eddy settled in to get a few winks.

But sleep evaded him. Though his body was tired, his mind was busy. On the drive from their home to the airfield ten minutes away, Maria had again brought up the subject of flying. This time with a new concern.

"Whose airplane are we borrowing? You said 'Mr. Smith's'; do you mean *the* Mr. Smith, or someone else?"

"That depends on who you mean by '*the* Mr. Smith,'" said Eddy.

"Oh, you know, the smuggler and arms runner."

"I think the man's character has been distorted. Sure, this Mr. Smith may be guilty of smuggling a few cigars from Cuba. Who isn't? Of the people who've been there, that is—and who smoke Cuban cigars. So maybe this fellow was caught once or twice—that immediately makes him a world-class smuggler who is arming the communists. This country is commie mad!"

"Have you ever met the man in question?" she inquired.

"Yes, actually, I have. We talked a great deal prior to his purchasing a pair of Bons."

"And?" Maria pressed.

"Well, he seemed like a decent enough fellow. Quite reasonable to work for. Intelligent. I'd say rather likable. Not to mention his impeccable taste in airplanes."

"I understand the Messerschmidts were good planes, but that did not improve your love for the Jerrys any. Perhaps choice of airplane is not the best indication of character."

"I s'pose not," Eddy shrugged. "But don't let this airplane bother you. I helped to design it myself—custom built for *the* Mr. Smith, and as safe as a baby's cradle! Now we have another prospective buyer who wants to see the craft. So Mr. Jensen and Mr. Smith worked out a deal, and here we are, on our way to California together. What more matters?" Eddy glanced at her while stopped at a light. She had been worried about being rushed out of the house without time to set her hair—a very silly worry in his opinion.

Now, gnawing at the back of Eddy's mind, a question presented itself: why had Milford's mechanic not wanted them to take the plane? He tossed the question about for a few minutes, and finding no answer, shrugged it off. Maybe he had not completed her oil change. Eddy could attend to that at their first fuel stop. Until then, he would get some much-needed shuteye.

It wasn't long before Eddy drifted off, though still in his subconscious he could feel Maria's head leaned against his shoulder. The temperatures dropped as the altimeter rose, and Eddy woke just enough to wrap his overcoat around Maria's shoulder and tuck her in. A glance out the window showed the mountainside below, cold and forbidding, snow drifting around the carpet of evergreens that stretched as far as the eye could see. This week, at least, they would bask in the warm sunshine and enjoy California's sandy beaches before returning to the Colorado autumn and settling in for the long, cold winter. Eddy closed his eyes and leaned his head back, the engine singing his lullaby.

But then the lullaby turned sour. Eddy tore off his headset to listen better as the engine grew louder, ominously choppy.

"I've lost all oil pressure!" the pilot exclaimed.

"Reduce power!" Jack commanded. His eyes scanned the gauges in front of him for scarcely fifteen seconds before giving his verdict. "We've got to get this Bon on the ground! There was an old Forest Service airstrip back a ways—turn about and we'll feather her in."

Carl unstrapped his lap belt and scrambled forward between the two front seats to take in the situation.

"You'd best get back to your seat," Jack cautioned. "This might be a bit of a ride."

"Yessir," Carl concurred. He looked over at Camille and smiled. Her face was drawn up in rigid lines. "Looks like we get a slight detour," he said nonchalantly.

Maria woke. "My ears are popping!" she complained. "Why are we—" She looked at Eddy. "What's wrong?"

He took her hand in his and squeezed. "We're having a bit of engine trouble: gonna put her down at an old airstrip." He felt her body stiffen, heard the sharp intake of breath as she looked out the window. Her perfect coloring drained from her face.

"Down? Here?"

All eyes in the cabin strained at the thick-forested, spiring mountainside, watching for the landing field. Several minutes went by.

"There it is! There it is!" Carl yelled.

"Hard to port!" Jack commanded. His days of rubbing shoulders with sailors as a fighter pilot on an escort carrier manifested itself in his choice of words.

They flew the length of the strip, checking for hazards. It was rough. A generous sprinkling of brush and evergreen saplings dotted the surface like whiskers, here and there a boulder jutted out its mossy chin; but it still beat ditching anywhere else.

"It's short," Jack cautioned. "Are you sure you have this?"

A nod from Westman, and pilot and passengers fell silent as the Bonanza turned the corner for final approach.

"Easy does it," Jack said. "Bring her around and set down as soft as you can."

Eddy's ears pounded as they had during his first solo. The engine was so rough—it couldn't go much longer. "Come on, girl," he whispered. "Keep going, keep—"

It sputtered and coughed, sputtered again, and gave out. Maria gasped and dug her fingernails into Eddy's arm.

"It's okay!" Jack said with authority. "We'll make it; we'll glide! We're gonna make it!"

They descended over treetops, the runway only two hundred feet beyond. The silence in the cockpit was now more deafening than the 165-horsepower engine had been. Walter gripped the yoke with white-knuckled intensity.

"Watch out!" Carl screamed. Too late. One tree, towering ten feet above its peers, caught their left wing and sheared it from the fuselage. The impact whipped the craft around, leaving the crumpled wing, and the Bonanza nose-dived toward the earth. It met the ground, flipped, and skidded eighty feet. A boulder stopped its slide and they came to rest on the corner of the abandoned strip.

CHAPTER THREE

A REAL PROBLEM

They had to get out—and quick! Eddy's hands ripped at the lap belt before his eyes were open, and he fell down the direction that should have been up. The world was a strange blur as he freed Maria's belt, unlatched the cabin door, and tumbled out. The smell of burning fuel stung the inside of his nose. He carried Maria, a flopping rag doll, through the brush and deposited her near a young pine sapling before returning to the devastated Bonanza.

Carl was struggling with Camille. She had seen the fire and was fighting like a wildcat to keep him from carrying her through it. When Carl saw Eddy, he grabbed her flailing hands and pushed her out into Eddy's waiting arms. She caught Eddy's neck and wouldn't let go, sobbing convulsions racking her whole body. They reached the pine and Eddy peeled her arms away in turn.

"Get ahold of yourself, Camille!" he said, and shook her. She stopped sobbing for a moment and he took her face between his hands, looking her straight in the eye. "Take care of Maria," he demanded.

She nodded, gulping twice. "Okay."

Eddy sprinted back to the plane. Carl was inside trying to free Westman of his harness. The buckle had jammed somehow, and the distressed pilot was wailing for help. Eddy pushed Carl's hands aside and tore it loose with one powerful yank.

"It's really heating up in here!" Carl yelled above the crackling flames. "Let's get him and go!"

Eddy reached his arms under Westman's and locked his hands over the pilot's chest. Carl got his legs and they jumped from the cockpit.

"All right, set him down," said Eddy as soon as they were a safe distance from the fire. The kid was in bad shape: it took no expertise to see that. Eddy's two years of medical school only highlighted the fact for him. Face ghostly, eyes wide and staring, frothy red sputum expelled in a cough; and then the more obvious: the raggedly torn shirt, sticky and glistening with crimson.

An agonized cry wrenched past the pilot's lips; his hand clutched at empty space.

Carl grasped the hand tightly. "Easy there, kid. I've got you."

Eddy yanked out his handkerchief. "Keep talking," he said, handing it to Carl.

"What about Jack?"

“I’m going to find him,” Eddy said firmly. He bobbed his head toward the pilot. “Stay with him.” He turned to race back to the flaming Bonanza. Still no sign of Jack. Circling the roaring bonfire, the glowing tongues of flame licking up the fuel, Eddy bellowed his name. He was seconds from diving back into the aircraft, when a shrill whistle stopped him. He turned, saw a pin-striped arm waving at him, and ran through the scrub until he came upon Jack, lying on his back, panting.

“Broken leg,” Jack explained when Eddy reached to help him up.

Eddy grimaced. “Couldn’t you have saved that for someone a bit lighter?”

“Gladly,” Jack returned. “Are you volunteering?” He grunted and stood, leaning heavily on Eddy. “How are the others?” he asked as they made slow progress toward Carl and Westman.

“Pilot’s bleeding real bad—messed up internally. Maria’s unconscious; I think she was out before we hit. Everyone else seems to be okay—a little shell-shocked.”

“A little? Hand me that stick and go tend to someone who needs your help!”

“But your leg—”

“Give me the stick!” Jack insisted. “I’ll make it on my own. Go on, get outta here!”

Eddy supplied Jack with the crutch and staggered over to Westman, his legs as sturdy as jellyfish tentacles.

"How's—" Eddy began, and cut short. His handkerchief, stuffed in the pilot's wound, was soaked clear through, yet the bleeding seemed to have abated. Carl sat on his haunches, the pilot's hand limp in his own. He glanced up at Eddy; dull eyes conveyed the needed information.

"You find him?" Carl asked.

Eddy nodded, and gestured briefly in Jack's direction before turning toward the landmark pine sapling where Camille and Maria waited.

"Here!" Carl husked the leather flight jacket from the body of its former owner. "You might want this."

Wordless, Eddy nodded and took the jacket.

ꕤ ꕤ ꕤ

They were killed. All six of them dead. And all due to Westman's insubordination!

Westman! Smith's grandson, dead!

That meant Ferguson had to skip town. He revved the engine of his beat-up Ford, shifted up a gear, and jerked through the intersection. Now he was on the straightaway. He pressed his foot on the gas pedal, eager to put as many miles as possible between himself and Milford Smith before the deadly news came out. His peripheral vision faded as he looked down the long stretch of road that led out of town and away from the clutches of the raving madman Smith would become. Consequently, he did not see the woman and her young son as they stepped off the sidewalk to cross the street half a block in front of him, until it was almost too late. He swerved violently to the right, missing them by a bare twelve inches. The Ford jumped the curb and connected with a street lamp. Ferguson's head connected with the windshield. He pulled himself back into his seat and found himself looking into the face of Officer Fitzwilliam. Angry Officer Fitzwilliam. Quite possibly livid Officer Fitzwilliam. Ferguson noted that it was not a good idea, when trying to escape town, to nearly run over the constable's wife and kid while he was watching.

"Benny Ferguson!" Fitzwilliam boomed. "A little too long at the bottle, perhaps?" He whipped out his notebook.

"Uh, no, Officer. I'm cold sober!" Ferguson protested.

"Oh, you are, eh?" Fitzwilliam leaned close and snarled: "Then why didn't you stop for my wife like any decent man would?"

"I'm sorry, Officer. I didn't see them: I was in a hurry—"

Officer Fitzwilliam was not impressed by this excuse. He grabbed Ferguson by the shirt collar and hauled him halfway through the window when a fellow policeman came to the rescue.

"Take it easy, Willy! Let him go! I said let him go!"

Fitzwilliam turned on his colleague. "Did you see what he did?"

"Yes, I saw! And I don't want to see you do something equally stupid. Now let him go: I'll handle this!"

Officer Reynolds turned to Ferguson and looked surprised. "Why, Benny Ferguson! I didn't know you were a drinking man."

"I haven't been drinking!" the mechanic insisted. "Officer Reynolds, this is a matter of life and death!"

"Yes, it came close, didn't it? I'll take your statement down at the station. Now, if you'll step out—"

"There's no time!" Benny shouted. He threw the Ford into reverse and hit the throttle. Officer Reynolds was obliged to jump aside to avoid being knocked over, and Ferguson shifted into gear and headed off.

Officer Fitzwilliam dashed for his patrol car. This time Reynolds was right with him. Forgotten for the time was the wife and kiddie waiting for their papa outside the soda fountain. In their sights was an old Ford pickup, blazing down Mainstreet at a speed approaching forty miles per hour.

"We've gotta get 'im!" Fitzwilliam snarled.

Reynolds jerked his head. "We'll get 'im."

Down Mainstreet. Gaining, gaining. Lights and siren. Fitzwilliam reached for his holster.

"Not yet," Reynolds cautioned.

The Ford swerved: a blown tire. The truck crashed through a board fence. Shingles flew. The patrol car pulled up; Officers Fitzwilliam and Reynolds stepped out, ready to overcome a fleeing mechanic. The pickup's trail plowed through the garden patch, leaving a bloody tangle of aged tomato vines, shattered melons, splintered cornstalks. The giant pumpkin was the last straw for the old truck. It remained unmoved by the Ford's dented bumper.

Standing to one side of their blazed trail, the white-mustached gardener's foot slipped from his digging fork beside a mound of carrots. Officer Reynolds nodded his official head. "Good morning, Solomon."

Mechanical, the gardener nodded back. "Mornin'."

Officer Fitzwilliam reached the truck's door handle and pulled. Ferguson fell out, white and shaking. "He'll kill me . . ." he moaned.

Reynolds found Ferguson's arm and pulled him up, supporting dead weight. Fitzwilliam grabbed his other arm. The mechanic's head bobbed between his shoulders, a red trickle starting from between his eyes. The officers heaved him into the back of their car.

From the house came a shuffle of tired feet and the tapping of a cane. "Solomon! Solomon! Are you out here?"

The gardener called back. "Yes, Mama, I'm right here."

"I heard something. Better check the sweetcorn: those deer may be at it again!"

"Yes, Mama. Now you get back inside and set down! I'll check."

Officer Reynolds opened the driver's side door, lifting his hand toward the old gardener. "Morning, Solomon."

He nodded back. "Mornin'."

Officer Fitzwilliam slipped into his seat. "Aggh!" His body convulsed.

"What is it?"

Officer Fitzwilliam pointed at the floorboards, buried in a pile of outsized, green summer squash.

ꙮ ꙮ ꙮ

A black BMW pulled up at the airport. The chauffeur got out and opened the door, standing to attention with precise military discipline. A thick cloud of tobacco smoke escaped and scattered to the breeze, followed by a deep, gravelly voice.

"Go—look around. See who's here," it said from within the clouded interior of the car.

"Jawohl, Herr Herschner." The chauffeur closed the door and scouted about the hangars. He was back within a few minutes. "There is no one here, Herr Herschner."

"Good," said the voice. A hand emerged from the Beemer to dust ash from the tip of a cigar. "Now go—get the plane ready."

"Jawohl, Herr Herschner."

Some minutes later, the chauffeur returned.

"There is a problem, mein Herr."

"Yes, what is it, Schultz?"

"I do not know. The airplane—she sputters."

"Sputters?"

"Jah, Herr Herschner."

"That is impossible. I told the nincompoop mechanic to have her in perfect working order. I want nothing to hinder me today."

"And that is the other thing, mein Herr: the nincompoop mechanic is not to be found!"

Herr Herschner did some sputtering of his own then, as he heaved himself from the smoky depths. He walked to the hangar with Schultz following. It was as the chauffeur had said—the hangar appeared empty aside from a large birdcage, several tool benches, and a 1920 Rolls Royce under a tarp.

"See, no one is here," Schultz reiterated.

"So it would seem," Herschner replied evenly, still scanning the hangar. Just then a loud shrieking called out to them.

"What goes up must come down! What goes up must come down!"

Immediately Herschner's hand gripped the Luger in his holster. "Who is there?" he demanded, flashing the gun from side to side.

"Oh boy, pastrami on rye! Pastrami on rye!"

Herschner motioned Schultz to the Rolls: the voice came from underneath.

"I know where you are—come out." The Luger barrel was trained in the direction of the car. Nothing.

"Come out, I say!"

Still nothing.

"Lift the tarp at my signal," Herschner whispered to Schultz. "I will give him one more chance." Then loudly: "Come out now or it will not go well with you. I give you five seconds."

"Do it yourself!" came the squawking reply.

"Five, four, three, two—"

At last the screecher showed himself. A short, dumpy, green-feathered body appeared from underneath the car and waddled out. Oscar fairly shrieked at the sight of the two strangers: "Pastrami on rye! Pastrami on rye!"

Herschner stared blankly at the mannerless parrot. "Insolent bird, how dare you address me in that way?"

Oscar waddled over to the man's foot and climbed aboard. "What goes up must come down! What goes up must come down!" he repeated, and bobbed happily as he whistled a pretty tune.

"Where is the nincompoop mechanic, you disgusting green feather duster?"

Oscar turned to song and sang lustily, though not strictly on key. "The landlubbers lie down below—below—below!"

Parrots are not known for their discretion, and Oscar was no exception. He left a spot of something on top of Herschner's shiny black shoe with a cry of "Whoopsey!"

"Do you know, little bird," Herschner said darkly, "that I could shoot you dead?"

Oscar was unperturbed by this offer, cocking his head at the Luger barrel. "Oh boy, pastrami on rye!"

Finding his threat toothless, Herschner glared at his soiled shoe while Oscar waddled off under the car again. "How bad is the airplane, Schultz?"

"I am not a mechanic, Herr Herschner, I cannot say."

"Will it fly?" Herschner asked, putting undue stress on each syllable.

"I think it will, mein Herr; but whether it will make us safely gone—"

"We will take a chance on that, Schultz. Whatever lies ahead can be no worse than what we leave behind. I may be a very rich man . . . if I am not first a dead one. Get the plane ready."

"Jawohl, Herr Herschner."

From underneath the car came the shrill tones of Oscar once more. "What goes up must come down! What goes up must come down!"

CHAPTER FOUR

BIRDSEED

Reality was beginning to sink in, seeping through the cracks between shock and adrenaline, and freezing into the cold, hard truth. Camille and Maria clung to one another; but as Eddy approached, he could see it was for Maria's comfort and not the other way round. Camille watched his approach, and though the word *panic* was blazoned on every feature, it somehow did not faze her voice. She bent her head and spoke low in Maria's ear, at which, Maria revived. But only for a moment. As soon as Eddy's arms reached her, she went limp.

"Here, honey, get this on. You'll feel a lot better." He draped her shoulders with Westman's jacket.

Camille caught one of the sleeves to help him and gasped. "But this—this belongs to—" She shuddered.

"It's on loan," said Eddy. He pulled on the zipper. Maria looked up and burst into tears.

"Eddy! Your face! You're all bloody!"

He reached up and rubbed blood from his eyes, then felt along his forehead. A small suface wound dribbled over his left eye; but the real danger was a gaping wound about the size of Texas hovering over his left temple. He winced at his own touch as he explored it with his fingertips.

"I'm okay," he said after a couple seconds. He repeated a phrase which his father had used on him as a young boy when he had fallen and cut his head, but which offered very little comfort to a child convinced he was dying: "Scalp wounds bleed a lot."

It had the same effect on Maria. Knowing then what she needed, Eddy pulled her to him and held her close while she cried. How close he had come to losing her once again! He had promised himself it would never happen a second time. One time was too many. Twice . . .

He squeezed his eyes tight shut and rested his cheek on her head, inhaling the comforting smell of her freshly washed hair. He plainly remembered the day, nearly six years ago. December 7, 1941: known to the rest of the world as the day the Japanese bombed Pearl Harbor. He was stationed in England with his RAF fighter squadron at the time, counting the days until his number came up for leave, and he could go home to be with his new bride. She was supposed to be waiting for him with her brother Brad, who was stationed at Pearl Harbor. When Eddy heard the news of the surprise attack, he was frantic. Pearl Harbor was bombed, ships sunk, men killed, the US at war—and he didn't care. The whole world could have exploded in a giant fireball and he would not have cared. All he wanted was to find his wife safe and sound.

As soon as his feet hit New York soil, he made a beeline for the West Coast. Maria, who had been delayed and never made it to Hawaii at all, learned through the grapevine of his coming and retraced her steps from California. By some miracle they met in Colorado, and there they had remained. Of course, Eddy had transferred to the United States Army Airforce, hopping all around the country, serving overseas; but their address had remained the same. Same town. Same house. Same post office box, even. A wonderful constant in their ever-changing world. And Eddy always knew he could come home and find his girl waiting for him.

"I'm sorry," he said at last to Maria. "I should have left you at home. Should have left you where you would be safe. Where you wouldn't have to face this."

She stopped crying suddenly and looked up at him, mascara leaving dark blotches beneath her eyes. "No." She shook her head. "I prefer to be with you. When you leave, I never know when you're coming back . . . *if* you're coming back. It's better to be here with you."

"That's my girl!" Eddy said, and kissed her on the cheek.

Camille opened Eddy's kit bag, which had been tangled in with Maria when Eddy had brought her from the plane.

"Let me do something for that wound," she suggested, reaching for a sterile dressing.

Eddy stopped her hand. "Later. Jack's got a broken leg," he explained as Jack and Carl made their way over to join the group.

"All present or accounted for," Jack commented, easing to the ground with Carl's help.

No one answered. Eddy glanced sideways at Carl, at Jack, and then again at Carl. His taut nerves snapped like a thread.

"Say it: go ahead and say it! I left the kid to die in your lap, not mine!"

Carl's eyebrows lifted together. "Someone had to go get Jack," he said evenly.

Eddy still looked from one to the other of his friends.

"Hit a bit of a rough spot on the way in," Jack observed to no one in particular.

"A *bit*," Carl agreed.

Eddy wiped a hand over his face. "All right. All right, Jack, do you want to do this or shall I?" he asked, fiddling a morphine syrette from its package.

"I don't want that stuff," Jack complained, flat on his back. "Give it to someone who does!"

"Unfortunately, you don't have any choice in the matter. Carl and I are going to splint that leg of yours, and you'll want it well enough then."

Carl grimaced. "I guess I don't get much choice in the matter, either."

Eddy shook his head. "Not much."

Jack took the syrette and stabbed the needle through his trousers and into his thigh, squeezing the contents from the tube. They had all carried morphine during combat, but even after sustaining machine gun wounds to the abdomen, he had not seen fit to use it. Now he would spoil his record over a broken leg.

"We've got about twenty minutes before that takes effect, so Carl, see if you can find a couple straight limbs for a splint. You just take it easy, Jack. I'm gonna check the plane—see if there's anything we can salvage."

"That fire's not done," Jack warned. "It's bound to be explosive: don't go near that plane, Eddy! You hear?"

Eddy called over his shoulder: "I hear you, Jack: you can court-martial me later!"

The Bonanza floundered on its back, landing gear helplessly reaching for the sky. Acrid fumes clouded the air, heavy and stifling with heat. Eddy skirted the tail and found the luggage compartment. It was locked. Of course! Why hadn't he thought to grab the key off Westman? No time for that now; he climbed into the backseat of the cockpit. The luggage had shifted and overflowed the cargo net in the convulsions of the flight, and was now a chaotic jumble. Eddy grabbed the handle of a bag—any bag—and yanked it free. He grabbed another. It was wedged between the seats and more luggage, and would not come loose.

Outside, the fire was looking for a new source of indulgence: the remaining right wing with its full tank of fuel.

A warning hiss, a threatening pop, sparks flying upward in greedy excitement. Eddy tried once more to jerk the bag free as a loud bang sounded. The bag remained unbudged. He gave up, grabbed a small duffle, and pulled it loose even as the wing exploded with a burst of flame. Tumbling backward out of the plane, Eddy landed on his back as more explosions followed. The harrowing memories of anti-aircraft guns booming and spitting their charges at his P-51 Mustang flashed vividly in his memory as he got up and ran.

Arriving breathless beside Jack just seconds before Carl, Eddy dropped the two bags he had recovered.

"You crazy Brit!" Jack exclaimed. "What are you trying to do? Kill yourself?"

"No, I'm trying to keep you alive," Eddy returned. "How're you feeling, Jack?"

He set his teeth and stared into the sky above. "Just do it."

"All right. Ready, Carl?"

Carl grimaced and nodded.

The break was a closed fracture midway between ankle and knee. With Carl supplying the needed traction, Eddy manipulated Jack's leg until it was as near to straight as he could make it. They applied the makeshift splint, well-padded with Eddy's overcoat, and tied it securely with belts and Jack's necktie.

"Are you done yet?" Jack griped, his voice raspy and gruff. Both hands were fistfuls of wet earth.

Eddy flopped down beside his patient. "I'm done. We coulda waited until that morphine had a chance."

Carl patted Jack's arm. "Good ol' Jack. Tough as boot leather," he added, trying to ignore the churning in the pit of his stomach.

Jack closed his eyes. "This ol' boot needs oiling," he admitted.

"We all do, if food and water, shelter—rescue—come under that definition," said Eddy. He glanced up at the sky, deepening in color with the approach of nightfall, the first stars shimmering faintly. "Looks like it's gonna be a cold one. We need to get a shelter up. Come on, Carl, let's—"

Carl gasped and moaned all at once. Eddy looked up sharply. Carl's face was sickly pale, his upper body leaned forward at an odd angle, his right arm tucked around his ribcage as though protecting a nest of eggs. The pathetic droop of his left shoulder spoke of pain with silent eloquence.

"Can't breathe!" he panted.

Eddy stood and guided Carl to sit down in his place. "Just concentrate on breathing, bud." He lifted Carl's shirt, felt along the ribs, felt the washboard unevenness of them. Fortunately no break in the skin.

"Broken ribs?" Carl gasped the question between shallow breaths.

Eddy nodded. "And that's not all. Raise your arm."

Carl gasped and nearly cried out with the attempt.

"Hmm. Fractured collarbone, I think."

"Thanks, doc . . . a little morphine?"

Eddy shook his head. "Not for you: it constricts breathing, and yours is rough enough as it is. Just concentrate on breathing in, deep as you can."

"Could at least die happy," Carl moaned.

But Eddy was unmoved. "Not a drop."

"You'd better sit down too, Eddy," warned Jack. "You'll be feeling it when the adrenaline wears off."

"That's exactly why I'm not sitting: somebody's gotta take care of you kids, and it looks like it needs to be me! Come on, Carl, breathe!"

ꕥ ꕥ ꕥ

"Excuse me," said Orville. "A man brought this for you." He eyed the battered biscuit tin, holding it at a distance from his body.

Milford sat in his chair, fingers laced together across his girth. He nodded. "Open it."

"Open it, sir?"

"Are you a butler or an echo? Yes, open it."

Orville took the tall container in one arm and pried the top off. "It . . . it's birdseed, sir."

Milford smiled. "Get a bowl, Orville. A large one." His eyes closed and his head began to nod.

"Will this one suffice, sir?"

Milford nodded. "Now dump it." He made a gesture at the tin. "Yes, all of it. Why must I spoon-feed you everything?" Milford downed the last of his drink and waited, eyes closed. Birdseed rattled against the sides of the metal bowl.

"How extraordinary, sir!"

Milford's spine snapped straight. "What is it?"

"It's . . ." Orville lifted the stub-end of a thick cigar. "It's still warm, sir."

With a yell, Milford struck the cigar from Orville's hand; the butler's arm collided with the bowl and sent it spinning across the table. It reached the edge and toppled, spraying millet, colliding with a brass lamp and knocking it over.

Orville gasped and went to his knees. His hands scooped the seed back into the tin. "Sorry, sir. Didn't mean to—"

"Go. Go!" Milford flicked his hand and sank back in his chair. "Never mind that now."

"Terribly sorry, sir."

"It was a failure."

"Too bad, sir." Orville picked up the cigar stub from the maroon-patterned rug.

"Give that to me, Orville. He must think I'm as much a fool as I think he is." Milford guffawed and held the end under his nose. "Ugh!"

CHAPTER FIVE

HOT COFFEE!

A small campfire crackled heartily, helping to lift the spirits of the four survivors who sat around it. Eddy had assigned Camille the trying task of making sure Carl remembered to breathe and insisting that he inhale deeply at least once every five minutes. At the same time she fashioned a sling with her head scarf, securing his arm to his chest to ease the load on his collarbone.

They had relocated up the hill a short distance from the airstrip. There the mountain had been cut by runoff, forming a ravine with a slight overhang of bare rock. A shelter, at least, from the chilling wind. Despite this, the fire, and Westman's jacket, Maria's teeth chattered uncontrollably in a sort of jittery Morse code. Jack lay at full length by the fire, the morphine having taken full effect.

"We've got water close by," said Eddy, leaning forward as he came up the slope. "I heard it coming down just west of here." His footprints were erased by a long curving pine branch that dragged the ground behind him.

"What's that for?" Camille asked.

"This is the beginning of a roof," he explained, drawing the bough across the dugout. It wasn't much. He would add the needed smaller branches, sticks, leaves, and other debris to complete it later. "How's Carl?"

"Let me die," Carl answered.

"Good. Still breathing. Keep him jabbering, Camille: the more he talks, the more he's gotta breathe." Eddy knelt by Jack and took his hand.

One eyelid peeled back briefly. "Don't worry about me, Eddy."

"I'm not," said Eddy, checking Jack's vitals. Satisfied, he turned to Maria, coming behind her, wrapping his arms about her delicate frame. "How are you, Maria?"

"I hurt."

Eddy's stomach lurched. "Where?"

"Everywhere," she said, trembling.

"You're going to be sore, darling. But that's okay: it'll wear off. Just so long as you don't think there's anything broken. You're going to be okay. We just need to get you warmed up." He looked around. Underneath the tree canopy it was getting dark. They needed to think about bedding down, getting something to eat . . . and then just living through the night. If they managed that, they would work on signaling for help in the morning. He opened his kit—everything meticulously organized—and removed the mess tin. Sloshing the water in his canteen to measure it, he poured water into the tin, setting it on a rock by the fire. Two beef bouillon cubes plopped into the water, and the wrappers curled and disappeared into the flames. It would be very watery stew tonight, but at least it would be warm.

Carl watched Eddy's preparations through almost unblinking eyes. "You don't have the mess cups to go around," he muttered, half to himself.

"If you had thought to bring your kit you could have helped that situation," Eddy said acidly.

Carl let it pass and breathed in painfully at Camille's urging.

Leaving his dinner preparations for the time, Eddy turned to the two bags he'd salvaged earlier. He opened the suitcase: Camille's, obviously, for it was packed with several skirts and blouses, a makeup case, two pairs of flat-soled shoes, and various other frills she no doubt did not care for him to see, much less paw through. Eddy stole a glance at her while she studiously avoided looking his direction, her cheeks showing a blush of pink as she finished with Carl's arm.

Eddy dropped the suitcase lid, muttering. "Not a sweater, not a jacket. Not a stitch of anything useful."

"I was going to California, not Antarctica," Camille said. Her voice quavered with a hint of tears. "And I didn't intend to spend the night in the mountains, either."

Eddy took a deep breath and unzipped the duffle. On the side were the initials WJW embroidered in blue, and in it, shirts and trousers, socks and underclothes, a small toiletry bag—the bare essentials.

"The kid packed light," Eddy commented. He took a pair of trousers and handed them to Maria. "Put these on."

"You should have grabbed my bag," chided Carl. "I *did* bring my kit: emergency rations, medical supplies—it was all in there."

"You should have been there to show me which *was* your bag with the airplane blowing to pieces in *your* face!"

"It was the army-issue duffle with my name on it," Carl said loudly, forgetting his ribs for the moment. "I put it on top in case we might need it."

"If you will recall," Eddy hissed, "the plane was upside down—anything you put on top was on the bottom! I had a hard enough time getting these."

"Yeah, and a lot of good it's done us, too! I don't suppose you thought to check the radio!"

The radio! How could he have forgotten? It would be of no use now. Whatever had survived the crash was surely destroyed by the fire. Mentally chastising himself, Eddy vented a little steam: "Do you expect me to do everything? Here you are, sitting by *my* fire, complaining about your ribs while I'm trying to do all I can to help! Why don't you get up and do something useful?"

A long, painful silence followed. Carl looked down and drew circles in the dirt with his finger. Camille turned her back to the campfire. Maria watered the pilot's sleeve with her tears.

Eddy felt sick. He had deftly sliced through the artery of morale, allowing the contents to bleed out. Surely they would have better chances of survival without his blundering, forgetful, frustrated presence?

Jack's voice, calm and soothing as ever, graciously saved the moment. "It won't do any good to point fingers at each other. We're all in this together: that means we all live together or we die together. How many times, Martin, did you have a Jerry on your tail, and your buddy shot him off? And how many times did you do that for him?"

Eddy was silent.

"You can't count the times," Jack continued. "You *don't* count them. No one keeps score—you just give it all you have and when you've given all, hopefully the others can take the slack. If you all want to get out, you all have to work together."

Well done, Doctor Jack! With the artery successfully tied, perhaps the patient could live. Eddy drew in a long breath. "I'm sorry, Carl."

Carl looked up and smiled sheepishly. "Yeah, me too."

The water in Eddy's mess tin was starting to dance. Glad for the diversion, he took it from the fire and poured half of it into his cup.

"Did you . . ." Carl spoke softly so as not to reopen the recent sore. "Did you happen to check the radio?"

Eddy shook his head.

"Well, it was probably dead. Probably didn't survive the crash. We hit hard."

Eddy agreed, and for the hundredth time tried to remember his crash at an RAF field in England. He had put down hard, he knew, because it had bent up his Hurricane's landing gear. Yet no one had faulted him, considering he had five bullets in his chest.

Jack interrupted Eddy's reminiscing. "I guess I owe you all an apology," he said. "I'm afraid the blame for this crash rests squarely at my door."

"Oh no, Jack!" Camille exclaimed, and the others were quick to chime in with like sentiments.

"It couldn't have been your fault, Jack," Carl said firmly, now as quick to defend Jack as he had been to tear into Eddy a few moments earlier. "No one could have foreseen the oil pressure dropping like it did."

"No," Jack sighed. "But I had a hint of a warning when the mechanic called in, telling Westman to ground her. As senior officer, I should have taken the initiative to make him turn back."

"I heard that warning, too," Carl put in.

"And I heard it from Carl," Eddy added. "We're all equally guilty here, so like you said, Jack, it won't do any good to point fingers. What's done is done." He paused. "So how 'bout dinner?"

"I'd be happy for dinner," Carl said, looking dubiously at Eddy's sparse preparations. "But that don't look like it."

"Well, it's something," said Eddy, passing their one cup around. They each drank eagerly, glad for warmth and taste even if it was not actual food.

"We have much to be thankful for."

The suddenness of the expressed sentiment caused all heads to turn in Jack's direction. A blank silence stretched between them.

"Yeah." Carl eyed the empty cup before passing it back to Eddy for a refill. "Yeah, I guess we do."

Eddy reached for Maria's hand, one corner of his mouth lifting in a half smile.

As if by mutual agreement, heads bowed, eyes closed, and thanksgiving was raised to the One who, having given them life, had seen fit to preserve it, and even sustain it with food for the moment. Perhaps not surprisingly, the plain broth tasted better, the fire seemed warmer, as did the company. For a moment, physical pain was forgotten in the grateful pleasure of being still alive.

ꕤ ꕤ ꕤ

Still alive . . . For what? Jack's mind skimmed the past six years. Long and lonely: six years since he and Pearl . . . But no, he could not think of it. Not here. Not now. Absently, his fingers touched his buttonhole: the place where his gardenia should have been—*would* have been, had not all this . . .

But the fact remained that he was still alive. To what purpose? He looked at Eddy: handsome and eager. And Carl, quick and capable. Camille was young and shy and sweet. Beautiful Maria had always been good to him, and to Eddy as well.

It could be the answer to his perennial question lay in their current predicament. Why had his life been spared, if not for this very time: to help save the lives of his friends?

❧ ❧ ❧

Carl wiped the back of his hand across his mouth. "That's good stuff, Martingale, but when do we eat?"

"Tomorrow," Eddy said firmly. "We've got more bouillon, biscuits, Spam, and your favorite: chocolate soap bar. But that's all for tonight. I haven't quite figured out the ration yet, but to last a week, between the five of us . . ."

Maria looked startled. "A *week*?"

"That's a worst-case scenario, Maria. We've got to be prepared for whatever comes."

"*Just* a week, Eddy?" Carl asked.

Eddy looked down for a moment. "Just a week, Carl. We'll be out by then—one way or another . . ." He paused and looked up again, taking on a more optimistic expression. "Of course, we can always supplement our diet: we might find some late-season berries, trap some rabbit, or . . . Aren't pine needles edible?"

Carl was quick to pop one in his mouth. "Not especially good," he said, and spat it out.

"You'll like them better when you're hungry," said Eddy, clearing up the dinner things. "If anyone has any special in-flight rations, let's see them."

Everyone shook their heads mutely. Then with an exclamation, Camille reached into her skirt pocket and withdrew a small handful of peppermint candies. "Flying always makes me a little queasy," she explained, handing them over.

"Anything else?"

Maria and Carl both shook their heads.

Jack opened one eye. "I have no food," he said. "But what I do have is lying in the small of my back and goes by the name of Wesson."

"At least we have that," Eddy said soberly. "Though I wish for all the world his name was Springfield." His voice got quiet as he gave the news. "I saw cat tracks. Fresh. And big."

ꙮ ꙮ ꙮ

Inspector Rigby hated to eat and run—but of course, he was a very busy man, so it could not be helped. No, he could not possibly stay for dinner. Lunch had been delicious, as had the early afternoon snack. What's that? Tea and cookies? Mouth watering. He couldn't, really. But if Milford insisted . . .

The inspector finally dragged himself away. He returned to his car to find his driver snoring behind the wheel.

"What's this, man? Sleeping on the job?"

The driver pulled himself up straight and started the engine. "No sir. I don't sleep and you don't eat. Where to, sir?" he asked with a yawn.

"To headquarters," Rigby growled. "I've got to write a report on this guy: there's enough stuff on him to bust him wide open once and for all."

Now in truth, all Rigby had on Milford was a large gravy stain neighbored by a pink smear of raspberry preserves—and it was *he* that was about to bust wide open. But when one has spent part of the morning and a great deal of the afternoon in pursuit of any good reason to lock a gun-smuggling, commie-dealing, biscuit-eater behind bars, and has come up with a lot of nothing (excepting a bad case of indigestion), one does not like to admit it. And so he didn't. If only there were a law prohibiting the calculating of ridiculous mathematical equations concerning bathtubs full of holes. Unfortunately, Rigby was unaware of any such law in the books. And so Milford was safe in his mansion scribbling on his calligraphy tablet.

It was two thirty when they arrived at the station. Rigby waddled in and went for the break room to fix himself an Alka-Seltzer. A couple of the boys were there already, muttering over steaming cups of freshly brewed coffee. They did not look happy. Barely noticing Rigby's presence, the first one kept talking to his buddy, his voice getting louder as he spoke.

". . . and by that time, I didn't care who he was: if he'd been President Truman himself, I still woulda hauled him outta that car and snapped his little neck!"

The second officer laid a hand on his friend's sleeve and nodded in Rigby's direction. Rigby drank his stomach tonic and began to feel its calming effects, ignoring the intense conversation of the boys in blue until it once more got out of control.

"I don't care if he says someone's out to get him! I wouldn't care if he had an army of fire ants marching up and down his backside! Whether he's insane, blind, or just plain stupid doesn't make a bit of difference: he's a danger to the public—and men like him oughta be locked away for a long time!"

Rigby decided coffee would be nice after the strenuous afternoon, selected a thick china cup, and started to pour.

The cop continued. "And as for this smuggler, arms dealer, whatever-he-is Smith, I don't care . . ."

That was all Rigby heard. At the mention of smuggling and Smith in the same sentence, Rigby looked up. "Smith? You don't mean—Yipes!" Scalding coffee streamed over the back of his hand. Rigby's yelp matched an opera soprano's. He dropped cup and pot, the latter shattering on the floor. Waving his hand vigorously, he rushed to the sink to splash it beneath a stream of cold water. When the burning had sufficiently subsided, he looked over his shoulder to explain his bizarre actions to the wondering policemen.

"Coffee's hot!" he said with a nervous grin.

Yes, they nodded in agreement. Very hot. They sipped carefully.

"That fellow you mentioned—the smuggler?"

"You've heard of Milford Smith," said the second officer.

"That's my man!" Rigby exulted, turning off the water and drying his hand. "Milford Smith—you got a friend of his?"

"Yeah," said the first. "His airplane mechanic: goes by the name of Benny Ferguson. A real creep! Goes speeding through town intent on murdering helpless pedestrians!" The hand was on his arm again.

"Cool it," said the second officer. "I suppose if you wanted to talk with him you could get down to the interrogation room," he said to Rigby. "They've been down there for an hour already."

"All right. Thank you," Rigby replied, and rushed for the door.

* * *

Maria was a sight, to be sure. Outfitted in a pair of Westman's oversized trousers, her blue-and-white polka-dotted dress over that, and Westman's jacket over that, the look was completed by a pink cotton nightgown turban. And still, she shivered. She watched listlessly while Eddy patiently worked a third pair of socks onto her little feet.

"All right," said Eddy, giving one last tug. "Now let's get you to bed." He led her to the back of their dugout where he had hollowed out an area for a bed and lined it with all the extra clothing they had. It was not much, but possibly with the two girls sharing body heat they would not freeze.

Eddy glanced over his shoulder at Carl and Camille, still sitting by the fire, impatient for Camille to join Maria.

"Go on, Camille; better get to bed," Carl advised.

"All right. But you'd better breathe!"

"I'm breathing," he muttered.

"Just see that you continue to do so," Camille smiled. She rose stiffly and moved toward the bed, then paused and looked back. "Carl? Tell me, do you think we'll make it out?" Her searching eyes scanned his face for any sign of hope.

Carl reached for another stick and tossed it onto the fire. "Sure," he answered. Then finally, he looked up again. "Sure, we'll make it."

She held his gaze for several seconds and shook her head. "You're a poor liar, Carl. That's okay. I wouldn't like you half so well if you were a good one. Goodnight."

"'Night," Carl said dully. He watched her crouch her way to the back of the dugout, then turned again to the fire. "Plane crashed, pilot dead," he murmured. "One broken leg, and a bloody head. Summer moved out, winter moved in, and now the future looks rather grim."

He shook his head, disgusted that he could sit there making up rhymes at a time like this, and partly because his last couplet was not a rhyme at all.

His mesmerized eyes reflected the dancing glow of flame. But his mind was elsewhere. His first assignment. Germany. After an intensive training period, he and his team were parachuted into the back country. Rugged, steep, cold. Unforgiving. Within a week, their medic had torn a ligament in his knee. Then McKenzie gashed a hole in his leg and was fighting infection. The loss of supplies and a navigational error sent them backtracking nearly two days' travel, and then trying desperately to remain on schedule.

But that was not the worst of it. Still vivid in his memory, he heard the gunfire—so sharp and clear that he started and glanced about. He could still see the bewildered faces of his comrades as they were led away at gunpoint while he watched, helpless against the odds, from the brow of the hill.

An information leak; the enemy had known their whereabouts and were ready and waiting for them to fall into the trap. The jaws had closed, missing Carl and McKenzie by inches. But poor McKenzie had not lived to see US soil again. In just two weeks, he had succumbed to the rigors of the mountains. And Carl was alone.

"You going to bed?"

Carl glanced up to see Eddy standing over him. "No . . . no, not me; couldn't sleep if I tried."

Eddy knelt and felt Carl's pulse. "How's the pain?"

"Fine, thanks for asking. How's yours?"

Eddy ignored Carl's sarcasm. "I thought it must at least be bearable—but then you stopped complaining and I began to wonder." In the absence of a stethoscope, Eddy leaned forward and placed his ear against Carl's back to check his breathing.

"I thought my complaining bothered you," Carl said, gritting his teeth.

"It was beginning to get on my nerves," Eddy admitted. "But your silence is worse—thought something must be really wrong." He paused and listened intently, then shook his head. "How in the world did you enlist with lungs like that?"

Carl smiled wanly. "Just had to convince the Allies they couldn't win without me."

"Ah. The boys in the enlisting department were desperate—or gullible. Give me another big breath."

"Don't be funny, doctor," said Carl, commencing a series of short, sharp gasps.

Eddy sat straight again and shook his head. "I can hardly tell if you're breathing or swimming in there. Ever had tuberculosis?"

"No."

"Pneumonia?"

"An old friend of mine."

"Well, he's no friend of mine, so he can't stay. Carl! What am I gonna do with you? Wish I had some penicillin, and something for the pain . . ."

"It's okay, Eddy: I'll be all right. I'm not done yet—I've had it worse before."

Their eyes locked for a solemn moment and then Eddy nodded. "I know, Carl." He paused. "I'm not worried so much about you yet. Nor Jack, for that matter. It's—" He stole a glance at the back corner of their dugout where the girls were sleeping.

"You worry enough for all of us, Martingale. She'll be okay. You get some rest; I'll take first watch." Even as he said it, Carl felt himself start to shiver. But not from cold.

Eddy took one look at his friend and declined the offer. "You need to lie down, Carl." He brought Westman's duffle for Carl to use as a pillow and helped him into the most comfortable position possible.

"Try to get some sleep. We'll be signaling in the morning—maybe we can get out of here." Eddy pulled Jack's pistol from his belt and checked it over as he settled in for his watch. The metallic click of the slide was a comforting sound to both of them.

There's no way I'm gonna sleep, Carl thought to himself with an involuntary little moan. He closed his eyes.

Plane crashed, pilot dead.
One broken leg and a bloody head.
Summer moved out, winter moved in.
Hope of rescue seems fairly thin.

ꟷ ꟷ ꟷ

The walrus-faced man behind the spectacles appeared grimmer than usual; his thick jowls wiggled as he tossed the final fresh grape into his mouth and sucked out its juices.

"You are tired, Herr Linder. Tired and weakening."

Carl stood hunched, the smart of his back no worse than the pinch in his stomach.

"But you need not go on in this way; in the end it will be of no use. Our methods have cracked better men than you wide open." He slurped deliciously.

That smell. Coffee? Carl's head bobbed down between his shoulders. The hand caught him from behind, crushing the nerve in his neck, shaking him ragged.

"We will continue where we left off yesterday, Herr Linder. The list of names, your contacts . . ." He lit a cigar and puffed on it in exaggerated pleasure.

Carl jerked his head in a sidelong glance toward the door.

Walrus noticed the gesture and his face flared with ghastly humor. "No, we do not wait for Herr Lubenstein today. He has given us already the information we ask of him, and as promised, has been set at freedom."

Carl's mouth fell open, trying to encapsulate the thought. Gerhardt free?

"But if he—"

"Herr Lubenstein was wise to tell us everything and has been released. He has been escorted to safety and will wait out the war in peace and comfort. You too, must pay the price—though it hardly matters now, since we know . . ."

Carl gasped, a little moan of desire. A few names. Then peace and sleep and silence. What did it matter? Carl opened his mouth and then clenched it shut, biting his tongue, making it bleed. Released? Ha! The ugly revelation stood out clear in the murk. Gerhardt was dead. Their torture had killed him. What was more, he had gone to his death in silence.

A clever ploy, a tempting offer. Carl closed his eyes. Death was still sleep. Perhaps it would not take long.

"I don't know what you . . ." The words coagulated on his thickened tongue. "I don't understand . . ."

"Still not very bright," said the walrus man, rising. He came around the desk, circled Carl, and paused to blow a cloud of smoke in his face . . .

ꟈ ꟈ ꟈ

Carl woke in violent coughing. Pain: relentless fire coursed through every nerve in his side and shot its needly spines into his shoulder and arm. The wind was sucked out of his lungs and he made a panicked attempt to sit up and catch his breath. Finally rolling onto his side, he used his good right arm to push himself into a sitting position. Several minutes passed before his spasmodic breathing evened out. He glowered at the smoking campfire.

Across from him, slouched against the dirt wall, Eddy's head sank down toward his chest, bobbing and jerking a little. And no wonder. It was nearly 0430 by Carl's watch. Eddy had been sitting up for seven hours. Time for him to have a break.

"Hey Eddy. Eddy! Why don't you go lie down. I'll sit up for a bit."

Eddy started and looked up, but not at Carl. His eyes stared hard, fixated on something in the night.

"Eddy? What's out there? What do you see?" The prickle of rising hair tickled the back of Carl's neck.

Silent, Eddy stood up and strode out from the circle of firelight. A new fear gurgled up from the pit of Carl's stomach and he jumped up and plunged into the darkness after his friend.

CHAPTER SIX

JUST GO UP

Eddy crouched in the brush, heart a wild drumbeat in his ears, pearls of sweat rolling off his forehead. It was a flier's worst nightmare: shot down over enemy-occupied territory, without the support of the squadron. And lost.

Already he had dodged one patrol. But they would be onto him soon enough: their dogs would catch his scent before too long, and if he was not many miles away by then . . . he was history.

He got up again and tore blindly down the slippery slope of the mountain, tripping over fallen logs and hidden stumps, plowing through tangles of branches that raked the insignia patches on his uniform. Behind him, he could hear the voices of the dogs, excited and eager. Then shouts from the men. They were onto him. He doubled his pace, flying down the hill. Then he lost his footing and fell headlong. He hit tucked, and continued head over heels: sky and ground, for thirty feet. Scrambling behind a sheltering tree, he crouched. One soldier was close on his tail. He had no dog, no comrade close by. If Eddy could not outrun them, maybe he could pick them off one by one. He coiled for his spring.

ꟷ ꟷ ꟷ

"Eddy! Eddy, stop!" Carl yelled into the pudding-thick darkness. Every breath was a knife in his chest, plunged in and twisted out; his side a spasm of pain. He had to stop and rest. He sank to the ground, muttering in German. Still his best thinking was in German. "What're you doing? What's wrong with you, Eddy? You gone crazy?"

Several minutes passed. He heaved himself to his feet and staggered forward again. A few short steps and he halted: he could not go farther. He paused to lean against a tree. A sudden movement, and a pair of hands clenched on his throat with an iron grip. Carl instinctively reached for his attacker's head. He grabbed a fistful of hair and ducked his shoulders, hurling him over with a well-practiced throw. They somersaulted together and landed with jarring force, Carl on top. Three whole seconds he lay stunned before rolling to his feet.

"Eddy, you idiot! Are you trying to kill me? Cause you pretty near did it!" He choked on a breath and the tears rose in his eyes. His body was screaming even if he wasn't. "This is serious! And your stupidity doesn't help!" He ran a shaking hand through his hair, willing himself calm, adrenaline and anger standing opposed. "This isn't a game, Eddy!"

But Eddy was not playing. He lay inert where he had landed; his eyes open, but dazed and expressionless. Carl knelt down: his raging emotions conquered by a sudden concern.

"Come on, Eddy, get up. Let's get back—"

Eddy sparked back to life. Eyes and mouth flung wide, he scooted away from Carl like a crab, scrambling to get to his feet. Carl made chase and reached to stop him. "Get ahold of yourself, Eddy!"

It occurred to him too late that he should not have spoken the phrase in German. Eddy whipped Jack's Mr. Wesson from his waistband and leveled it at Carl's face. Carl stopped dead and contemplated the largeness of the gentleman's nose, not two inches from his own, the black hole of the barrel holding his eyes in a hypnotic stare. When he next spoke it was in careful English.

"Eddy, it's okay. It's all right; just—just relax. It's me, your old friend, Carl Linder. Remember me, Eddy? Just take it easy now. Lower the gun. Put the gun down, Eddy. Just put it down . . ."

A light of recognition flickered in Eddy's eyes. He flung the pistol from him and sank his head into his hands, sobbing.

"Carl! I don't know what's wrong with me!"

"Well, I do," Carl said, starting to breathe again. He knelt by his friend, careful to secure Wesson in his own belt. "You've got a goose egg on your head that's gonna hatch an ostrich here pretty quick." He felt gently over

Eddy's head. "Maybe if someone had taken the time to look at your head before now, this wouldn't have happened. I was too busy worrying about how much I hurt . . ." Carl shook his head. "Come on, Eddy, let's get you back to camp now."

Eddy lifted his head long enough to pose a question. "Did we get them, Carl? Did we stop them?"

"What? Stop who?"

"The patrol; did we get them?"

Carl winced. "Eddy, listen: it's 1947. The war's over. No patrol came through here. You understand?"

"Then what . . . ?"

"We're in Colorado, Eddy. The Rockies. We were headed to California with the Bon for Beckett."

"The plane crashed," Eddy interjected.

"Right."

"And the pilot . . . he's dead, isn't he?"

"Yeah, poor kid."

"And Jack's leg is broken. You're all busted up . . . Camille and Maria . . . Don't even know what's wrong with me!" He paused to rub his head before looking up, on the verge of breaking down again. "We're never gonna make it out of here, Carl. There's no way we could ever make it: we can't walk, can't fly . . . No one knows where we are . . . we're just gonna die out here and be buried by the snow!"

Carl grabbed a fistful of Eddy's shirtfront and yanked him close to his face. "Shut up, Eddy! Shut up! Don't you go talking that way! You listen to me, Eddy, and you listen close: we're gonna make it out. They're looking for us, Eddy, and they're gonna find us. When we don't show up for that meeting today, you can bet your life that Mr. Beckett will be mad! And you better believe he'll ring up Mr. Jensen and give him what for! And when Jensen hears we're missing, why, he'll climb into the cockpit and come looking for us if he has to tie a sick-sack over his mouth! Don't you ever say we're stuck here, Eddy! I didn't come through the war to let this ol' mountain beat me; I intend to get back home and I intend to take you all with me!"

Eddy bobbed his head in agreement with each of Carl's points. "Okay. All right. Okay, Carl," he said with another nod.

"You got that, Eddy?"

"I got it."

"Good. Let's get you back to camp now."

"Wait. Carl? One thing."

"Sure. What is it?"

"Did we get them?"

Carl felt his stomach roll over."Eddy, it's . . . there's no . . ." He gave up. "Sure, Eddy. We got 'em. We got 'em real good."

"Okay," said Eddy.

"Let's get back to camp now. That wound on your head is broken open again—we'd better have Camille look at it."

"Okay," said Eddy, and stood up. Then he looked at Carl and frowned. "But . . . but . . . Camille?"

"Yeah, she's a nurse, you know. She'll know what to do for your—"

"But the nurses have been evacuated, Carl! Did they make it out all right? Did they—"

"Yes, Eddy! They made it out." Carl clapped an arm around Eddy's shoulder and started walking him toward camp, talking reassuringly. "They got out fine, Eddy. Now let's get back to the aid station."

"Okay," said Eddy. They started to climb the hill together. The going was slow. Eddy was wobbly on his feet, and when he wasn't tripping over something, Carl was. After fifteen minutes of arduous travel, Eddy pulled up short.

"I'll wait here, Carl. You go ahead and get your arm fixed. I'll sit down and rest for a minute." He sank down and put a hand to his head. Carl was helpless to stop him.

"No, Eddy!" Carl fell to the ground with him. "Ouch! Eddy, come on; you've got to come, too!"

"No, it's all right," Eddy insisted. "I'll take a short nap and when you're ready, I'll walk you back to the line."

"But Eddy, you've got to come too; you're bleeding."

"I am? Oh. That's okay—it doesn't hurt much." He rubbed his left bicep with his hand, remembering the wound he had sustained nearly three years ago when he and Carl had first met on the front. Eddy had saved his life then—carrying Carl five miles to an aid station. Of course, in the mere act of being there and needing assistance, Carl had quite possibly saved the life of the grounded flyboy; Eddy was as lost as a mouse in a snake's hole on the ground. Forget north and south: the only direction Eddy knew was up.

"Listen to me, Eddy, you'll bleed to death unless you get help!" Carl could not remember a time when it was imperative to convince a man he was mortally wounded. He had held McKenzie's head as the boy lay dying, telling him over and over again that he would be okay. This one was new.

Eddy looked up at Carl in surprise. "It's just a flesh wound—it will be all right."

"Eddy," Carl tried again. "You have to come with me—"

Eddy's face darkened. No one was going to tell him to do anything. "Carl!" He pointed a belligerent finger at his friend. "I am tired. I am going to sit down here and rest for a bit—and not you or anyone else is going to stop me!"

"That's what you think," Carl mumbled under his breath. "Fine. Just fine! You do that, I don't care. I'll see you later." He turned and marched up the trail a few paces before starting to gasp and wheeze loudly—an act not entirely forced.

Ah, poor, simple-minded Eddy, he thought to himself as the concussed pilot came to his aid once again. *If it weren't for his split head, he'd be downright predictable!*

Eddy knelt in front of Carl and loaded him onto his back piggy-style. "Which way?" he asked, getting to his feet.

"Up, Eddy," Carl said, allowing his head to flop over Eddy's shoulder. "Just go up."

ຣ ଓ ຣ

The police captain shook his head, laughed, and shrugged simultaneously. "Sure, if you really want to interview a nutcase." He jerked a thumb at the heavy door. "Go ahead."

"Thank you, Captain," Inspector Rigby nodded. He opened the door and paused for a moment on the threshold; two policemen were standing by the wall, smirking at each other. They straightened up and stood to attention as he entered. A pitiful morsel of humanity, the greasy airplane mechanic sat at the table, hands clasped in front of him, head bowed as though in belated prayer, eyes staring vacantly at a whirly knot in the wood. One could almost feel sorry for him. Almost. Rigby stepped forward briskly, confident and commanding as he addressed one of the cops. "Catch the light, would you?"

The patrolman glanced at his companion, who shrugged, and went to flip the switch.

"Benjamin T. Ferguson." Rigby switched on a bright lamp on the table. "You're in a heap of trouble."

Ferguson blinked at the sudden light and looked down.

"Well? Haven't you got anything to say for yourself?"

He shook his head.

"Tell me about it."

"I can't. He'll kill me!" Ferguson moaned.

"Who'll kill you? Who?" Rigby paused dramatically. "Your employer, eh? Milford Smith: the one who paid you to do it."

Ferguson paled. "How d'you know?"

"Because it's my job to know," Rigby bluffed. "So you wanna talk now?"

He shook his head again.

"Suppose, Ferguson, you have a chat with your employer, eh? How'd you like that? Would you like to share a cell with him for a couple of days?"

The mechanic's eyes widened until they resembled poached eggs—a lot of white with a bit of color in the middle. "No! He'll kill me!"

"Because you told? But you haven't said a word."

"He wouldn't care—he'd do it anyway!"

"Why?"

"Because I killed his—" Realizing what he had started to say, Ferguson flung back his chair and jumped to his feet, intent on making it out the door. The two men standing by dove after him, one getting a tackle hold round his knees, the other bringing him struggling to the floor.

"He'll kill me! He'll kill me!" Ferguson shrieked. He was beginning to sound more and more like a scratched record every minute, Rigby thought. He turned on the overhead light.

"All right boys, get him up."

They set Ferguson on the table, still holding an arm each.

"Listen here, Ferguson, you tell me everything and I promise he won't lay a finger on you."

"But . . . what will I get?" the mechanic asked, trembling in every limb.

"That depends on what you've done. But I'd say even the electric chair would be more comfortable than cement overshoes, wouldn't you?"

Ferguson wilted. Rigby thought possibly he would melt into a puddle and drip all over the floor. That would be a second mess he'd be responsible for.

"Tell me, Ferguson, and I promise you'll get a fair trial."

The mechanic nodded shakily. "All right. All right, I'll tell you. It started with two Beechcraft Bonanzas."

CHAPTER SEVEN

SHOCK

Helen Jensen pulled the car into the garage, being careful not to scrape the paint like she'd done last week. Harry had not been too happy about that. She turned off the car, shut the garage door, and walked into the house jangling the keys on her finger. Harry still wasn't eating, so she had enough time for a hot bath before supper—and after that, a book and bed. She started up the stairs to their room only to meet Harry coming out, tying his tie.

"Why Harry! What are you doing up? You must be feeling better."

"No. I feel worse than ever," he growled. "Fix me something to eat."

"Fix you something to . . . But darling, if you don't feel well, why don't you go back to bed? I'll bring up some nice hot tea and a slice of toast, and something to make you feel all better—"

Harry cut in. "Helen, they're missing." He finished his half Windsor with the skinny end hanging beyond his waist and pulled the whole thing loose to start over.

"Who?" Helen asked blankly.

"I just got a call from Cal Beckett: he said they never showed up for the meeting. He had a few other choice words, too, but they don't bear repeating."

"Cal Beckett: the California deal. You mean Camille?" Helen's brows knitted into a knot of worry. "But Harry, that doesn't necessarily mean they're missing," she insisted. "Maybe they were delayed by weather."

"I called about that—there was nothing that would have kept them from getting through. Even the mountain passes were remarkably fine today and yesterday both."

"Well, maybe they were confused by the time zone change," Helen suggested, unconsciously wringing her hands.

Harry paused tying his tie—which was now too long on the fat end, besides being twisted—to stare at his wife in disbelief. "Helen, it's Carl, Eddy, and Jack: they don't 'just forget' important meetings. And if they're confused about something, they figure it out. Besides, Camille would keep them on track better than that. And—" He paused before the clincher to look down at his tie again. It was hopeless. He unknotted it and let it fall. "And Mr. Beckett gave them an extra hour—if they were confused about the time, that should have sufficed."

"Harry, don't you—"

"Delays happen, I know. But if this had been merely a delay, I would have been notified by now. Their plane was supposed to get in yesterday, and I haven't heard a peep. I tell you, Helen, something's happened: they're in trouble. And so am I, if Camille's father or brother ever find out. If Amos were not paralyzed, I would be! Now what is there to eat?"

"I didn't fix anything for you, Harry. I didn't think you would be hungry."

"Well, what were you going to have?"

Helen looked down and stammered. "I—I was going to have the last piece of chocolate cake. But . . . I could split it with you . . ."

"Never mind that."

"But what are you going to do?"

Harry buttoned up his vest and put his jacket on as he spoke. "I'm going over to Smith's and see if he's heard anything. Then I'll report it to the police; see about getting a search organized."

"Will you be flying?"

"Yes."

"But Harry, don't you think you should—"

"Helen, I am going to find them, whatever it takes. You will not convince me to stay home; you will not convince me to wait until I feel better. Nor will you convince me to take any more of your nasty stomach tonic!"

"But Harry—"

"No, Helen. My mind is made up. I will go through hell and high water before I let those kids—"

She crossed her arms and glared at him. "Harry!"

"Well, what is it?" he asked finally, realizing she was not going to be so easily put off.

"Harry, don't you think you should at least put on some trousers?"

He looked down at his pajamas. Green-and-orange-striped pajamas. "Oh," he said. "Perhaps I'd better."

ꙮ ꙮ ꙮ

Seven pairs of church shoes sat by the front door, neatly arranged from smallest to largest. Camille hummed softly to herself as she completed her Saturday evening chore of smearing each toe with a bit of boot black and polishing until it took on a high shine. On any other day of the week, the locals might comment on the tattered Jensen boys, but never on Sundays. Socks, shoes, trousers without holes, shirts with no stains—Mama was always proud of how her wild brood of boys cleaned up for the day of worship. And Camille took her part very seriously. If it was up to her, each of her seven brothers would have the shiniest black shoes in the county.

And so she scrubbed away down the long row each Saturday night, singing an old hymn her mother taught her or trying her best to master the ever-elusive whistle that seemed so natural to her brothers.

One, two, three, four, five, six . . . where was seven? She stood up and looked around. The smallest pair of shoes was gone. But they were always promptly returned to their place by the door after Sunday morning service: anyone who was careless was at risk of a whipping. Had little Danny forgotten somehow? She looked behind the woodstove, on the bookshelf, under the kitchen table. No shoes. Where could they possibly be? Turning around once more, Camille noticed a big, strange box sitting in the middle of the room. Curious, she moved closer and lifted the lid. There was the seventh pair of church shoes, nestled in a wreath of daisies and goldenrod. They were no longer black and shiny, but scratched and scuffed: the polish flat. That would never do! Camille reached for the pair, intending to restore the black luster. But the heavy lid came crashing down on her hands, and the box disappeared in a flash. Vanished. Clean gone, and the shoes with it. Helpless, Camille sat down on the floor and cried.

When next she looked up, the line of shoes was changing: the shoes were growing. Camille stared in bewilderment as the size threes changed into sixes, the eights into tens. The nines became thirteens. Then the three biggest pairs were replaced with combat boots. Two smaller pairs were carried out in boxes. One pair became high-gloss officer's shoes. A pair of women's heels was added to the mix, standing toe to toe with a pair of boots; only to disappear again when the boots got flowers and a box.

The morphing continued through the week. Camille watched, powerless to stop it, held immobile by an invisible force until Saturday came again, and she got out her tin of polish and a rag. Only two pairs of combat boots remained. Then came a knock on the door. A man in uniform stood on the porch. He entered quietly, and took up the bigger pair, stuffing them into his overcoat.

"No, don't take them!" Camille pleaded. He shook his head without a word and pointed to the place where they had stood so many years by the door. There on the floor was the imprint of their tread, embossed in the floor as if it had been a bit of muddy ground.

"Will they ever come back?" Camille asked.

Still silent, the man picked up one boot of the last remaining pair. He placed it in a box on its own wreath of flowers, leaving behind its mate. He took a pair of crutches and leaned them against the wall beside the lone boot. Then he too disappeared. Once again, Camille sank to her knees and cried.

"It's all right, Camille. It can't last forever."

Camille looked up into the handsome, yet sad face of a uniformed man wearing captain's bars.

"This won't be forever," he repeated, and lifted her to her feet. Suddenly feeling like she had not slept in years, Camille collapsed into his arms.

"No, you have to be strong," he said.

"I can't, I can't! I'm done!"

"No." His eyes blazed through her. "No, you're strong. Just for a little while longer. I must go now—but I'll be back. And then you can rest." He steadied her on her feet and stepped back, watching to see that she could stand. His face warmed with a smile. Then, slowly backing away, his form shrank and shrank, and disappeared into a speck. She watched until it was gone, then stood looking around. Waiting for his return.

This is where the dream always ended: always waiting, hoping, wishing, praying. Never with the hope realized. Why could she never get beyond it? Why could she never find the glad ending she craved? She wrestled with her subconscious, trying to force it to continue, but the picture was fading, fading, and someone was shaking her awake.

"Wake up, Camille. Come on, wake up."

"No, I can't. I have to wait here."

"Come on, you've got to wake up."

"But I can't—" Camille opened her eyes, at once startled by the form of a man bent over her. The captain's? No—Andrew was broader, more muscular. And this man wore no uniform. It was Carl. She sat bolt upright.

"Are you all right?" Carl wondered.

Camille did a quick inventory: her left leg was a pain super-highway as all the signals marched up and down like an army on the move: she had forgotten to remove her brace. The rest of her body ached severely. It hurt to move; hurt to turn her head. About what you would expect after an airplane crash.

"I'm fine," she answered.

"Good." Relief flickered across Carl's face. His voice dropped in volume as he next spoke. "Would you come have a look at Eddy?"

Camille cast a quick glance at Maria and moved stiffly from their bunk toward the fire. Eddy was sitting near it, his knees bent, head drooping between them. The distinctly sickening smell of stomach acid assaulted her as she approached. Steeling herself, she knelt awkwardly.

"It's his head," said Carl. "He's got a big bump, bleeding, confusion . . . He didn't know me for a bit."

Camille nodded. She remembered the wound; the unconcerned way in which Eddy had written it off as insignificant. He'd fooled her. Perhaps he'd fooled himself as well.

"Eddy?" Camille lifted his chin, peering into his eyes. The variable firelight caught eerily in uneven pupils; a sight almost gruesome, other-worldly. Camille shuddered. "Eddy?"

The crazy eyes sought hers. "Cam. . . Cam—?"

"It's Camille, Eddy. Are you all right?"

No. Soundless, his lips formed the word. "My head hurts," he said. "Hurts pretty bad . . . Must have tripped, fallen or . . . or something." He rubbed the heel of his hand over his eye.

Carl leaned closer, squeezing Eddy's knee to get his attention. Annoyed by the gesture, Eddy brushed the offending hand away. "What do you want?" he growled.

"Eddy, what's your middle name?"

"My middle . . . What kind of a question is that? I'm in no mood for jokes, Sam." He shook his head. "What *is* my middle name? Hmph. Doesn't matter now . . . Oh, my head!"

Carl handed Camille Eddy's medical kit. "Here, you know what to do with this."

That's not true, Camille thought. She took the bag, fighting back tears. For three years as a volunteer in an army hospital, Camille had done such menial tasks as emptying bed pans, delivering meals, and offering words of comfort where she could. For three years, her work had been only the most lowly or detestable. Assigned the work other nurses balked at, she had changed the gangrenous bandages, tended the worst burns, scrubbed away the most revolting messes, and cried over each loss of life and limb. For three whole years, she had never set foot inside an operating theater except to clean it.

And now, in the middle of a medical emergency, the volunteer nurse was next to worthless. Her shaking hands opened the bag.

"Carl. I have a confession to make. I've never even—"

Carl looked up to meet her eye, but instead caught on the figure behind her: Maria. Carl went to her.

Maria shook her head, tears starting from her eyes. "No, not Eddy . . ." The words were hollow, barely more than a whisper, then rose in crescendo. "Not Eddy. It can't be Eddy! It's not—"

Carl had no time to waste on hysteria. Where reason failed, his arm would not: he drew it back and slapped her. She went rigid for several seconds, and then to Carl's astonishment, melted into tears.

"Sure. Make me feel like a heel," he muttered, settling down to the ground. "You just survived a plane crash, and you start to bawl when I slap you? I didn't even hit you that hard!"

Maria shook her head. "It's not that," she cried, her hand pressed against her stinging cheek. "It's . . . it's . . . oh Carl, I'm so scared!"

Carl nodded slowly. "Me too. Looks pretty bad for us. For Eddy . . . But he's taken care of the rest of us so far. As Jack said, now it's our turn. You've got to be strong for him, Maria. You've got to—"

"But I can't! I just can't! Not when he's like this, Carl." She looked up, expecting a sympathetic nod.

Carl's face held all the warmth of unpolished granite. "So let me get this straight: when you vowed to stand by Eddy through thick and thin, you really meant just thick, is that it? Well let me tell you, sister, this is rotten timing to let him know!"

Maria's eyes overflowed again and she choked on her sobs. "No, Carl, I don't—I don't mean that! I'll stick with him—I'll do whatever it takes."

"Good." Carl softened somewhat. "Then dry your eyes and get busy, 'cause someone else is doing your job." He nodded, indicating Camille: she had coaxed Eddy into the shelter and was urging him to lie down and be still so she could clean and bandage his head. Maria needed no more prodding, but got to her feet and went to see to her husband.

Carl took the opportunity to crawl off into the brush and die.

At least, that was what he wanted to do. He settled for climbing the bank and walking from the camp a good piece. Then he stumbled forward and fell to his knees. The world was a blur, and not merely from the rain that was starting to fall. He was going into shock, and declining rapidly: hands starting to tremble, each breath more a struggle than the last. A strange humming in his ears threatened to obscure outside awareness. He would not last long like this.

He shook his head, trying to clear it. "Come on, Carl! Get up! Get up: I know you can do better!" he berated himself. But his body would not respond.

"Survive the Gestapo's worst, and you're going to let this best you? Get up!" He sank to one elbow, not yet willing to fall on his face in defeat. *No, don't give up now!* Incapable of vocalization: his brain was going into concrete lockdown.

Then there was a strong presence beside him. Jack. Crutch, busted leg, and all.

"Carl, Linders don't give up so easily—I know this from experience." He got down in the dirt beside Carl. "Now don't make me carry you."

No. Jack, you can't. Your leg . . . Carl heaved himself to his knees again.

"Put your arm on my shoulder and I'll get you up. No excuses, soldier!"

Mechanically, Carl did as he was told. Jack struggled for some moments to find the wherewithal to lift them both, his body trembling as he rose. Suddenly Camille was there beside them, trying to help them both walk. She was telling Carl over and over that he would be okay: must be the thing you do when someone is dying.

Somehow they made it back to camp without falling. Somehow Carl was in bed beside Eddy. He was suddenly cold. He automatically moved closer to Eddy, then felt Jack near his other side. Camille was saying something, though he couldn't understand her words. His eyes closed. If he slept now, would he awake again? He didn't care.

CHAPTER EIGHT

THE SOUND OF WINGS

Carl's elbows rested on the worn bartop behind him. A shout from the street, and he adjusted the accordion in his lap; his arm began to manipulate the bellows, fingers gliding over mother-of-pearl keys.

A face appeared in the doorway, eager and searching. As the man behind it stepped into the pub, the tide of uniforms broke in behind him, filling the place in seconds with shouting, and laughter, and snatches of song.

Deutschland, Deutschland!

Carl started in with the first few notes. He was joined by men in the thrall of patriotic fervor, their voices owning Germany as the one, the only.

No offense to Haydn: it really was a pity to have his work co-opted with such words. But surely six feet of earth served as a suitable buffer between the composer and the sting of insult.

A coin flung in Carl's direction. He caught it, his other hand navigating unerringly through the end of the song.

The bright young corporal pulled up at the stool beside Carl's. He ordered two drinks. Carl nodded his thanks as one of them appeared at his elbow.

"How is the sickly patriot today?"

Carl smiled and shrugged, an answer glib on his lips. But talking was not his job. He moved the bellows rhythmically. A rowdy drinking song. The war-tired soldiers joined in.

There was Schmidt, Mullinger, Erhlich . . . From his vantage point at the bar, Carl scanned the room and planned his night's operations. Mouth flippant, ears keen. Keep the liquor flowing, keep the tongues telling. The sickly patriot at work.

༄ ༄ ༄

The first light of morning was already long gone when Carl next opened his eyes. Now, instead of cold, his body was awash with fever. Pneumonia. Or perhaps just the after effects of hitting the ground suddenly. He tried to take a breath. It was pneumonia, for sure. Carl struggled for a moment and sat up. Someone had taken the time to enclose their dugout with branches, leaving only a small doorway through which the light was streaming. It certainly made it warmer. Carl figured he was generating at least 50 percent of the heat. He raised a hand to his forehead and immediately jerked it away, surprised by the sudden meeting of chill and heat.

"How are you feeling?" Camille asked.

A long string of answers traipsed through his head. Terrible. Lousy. Worst ever. Don't ask. Let me die. He was favoring the last until he looked at her: she'd been through the wringer right along with him.

"I'll be fine," he said.

Camille smiled as one who recognized that reply for what it was. "Have an aspirin," she said, and measured three white tablets into his hand.

"But you'll need these," Carl protested wearily.

"I've had one," Camille said with a shrug. "Besides, it's just pain."

Yeah. Just pain. Carl knew what that meant. So did Camille. It had been a constant in her life since she was five, and the same polio that had carried off her baby brother held her in its grasp.

Camille handed Carl Eddy's canteen. "Take them, Carl. They help with inflammation, too."

"How much water have we got left?"

"Jack's gone for more. You needn't worry—"

"Crazy nut! He shouldn't be walking on that leg!"

"No," Camille agreed, "but he got the idea into his head and—"

"And there was no stopping him. That's Jack." Carl paused to swallow the aspirin. "Gentle as a kitten, stubborn as a mule—"

The sun was blocked momentarily as Jack came through the doorway with his crutch and a pot of freshly boiled water.

"—and happy as a tick on a dog's ear when hyped up on a second round of morphine," Carl commented at the sight of two empty syrettes pinned to Jack's collar.

"Somebody's got to take care of you kids," Jack quoted. "Figured it was my turn."

"One of those needles would be all the taking care of I need," Carl groused. He glanced over at Eddy, who was muttering incomprehensibly in his sleep. Beside him, Maria stirred and woke to adjust the pillow under his head.

"How's Eddy, Camille?"

Camille's thin shoulders lifted in a shrug. "I don't know." Her voice carried a peculiar note of dread. "He really needs a doctor."

"How bad do you think . . . ?"

"Don't ask me, Carl!" Camille said, more loudly than she meant. Biting her lip, she dashed a tear from her eye.

"At least he's sleeping," Jack observed.

Camille nodded. "I gave him some morphine. That has helped."

"Poor Eddy," Carl mused. "Best friend a fella could ask for. But you know it's fixin' to be a bad day when said best friend points a gun in your face."

Jack paused in filling the canteen to raise an eyebrow and pat the bulge on his hip: his handgun reclaimed from Carl sometime that morning. "Going above and beyond your usual calling of annoyingness, eh Carl?"

"I was not."

"Sure," Jack laughed. He poured the rest of the water. "I heard you singing your Wagnerian ballads all night. Why, it was enough to turn even *that* Englishman's ear!"

Carl laughed and cringed in spite of himself. "Camille, listen to him: he's had too much happy juice!"

But Jack wasn't finished.

"And finally, when the singing gave out and I thought I could sleep, who pulls out their accordion to give us some more Kraut Musik?"

"Give it a rest, Jack!" said Carl. "Why, if I had my accordion, I'd play you as fancy a polka as ever—" He stopped and looked down at his arm, bound tight to his chest. "Well, I'd teach *you* to play the polka—though perhaps it would cut our chances of rescue if anyone caught you practicing."

"Humph," Jack growled in mock offense. "I'd play you a polka and we would all waltz right out of here!"

"Waltz to a polka? What kind of three-legged klodhopper are you?" He held his side and grimaced against the pain, chuckling simultaneously. "Now honestly, Jack, what do you think our chances are?"

Jack did not miss a beat. "Not good if you can't waltz to a polka. Pretty bad since you forgot the squeezebox."

"Yeah, I must have left it in my other pants. Come on, Jack, what part of being serious don't you understand?"

Jack eased himself to the ground with a grunt. He stared at the toe of his shiny black dress shoe, now smudged with dirt. On impulse, he reached out and dusted the dirt off with fastidious care. When he looked up again, both Carl and Camille were waiting for his answer. His eyes returned to his shoe. "It depends on how badly you kids want to get out."

"On *us?*" Camille frowned. "But Jack, don't *you* want—"

"You never know what you can do until you try," Jack offered, regaining a touch of his former joviality.

"But Jack, don't you—"

"Hush!" Carl commanded. He cocked his head. "Hear that? Now there! Just listen." He squeezed his eyes shut and slackened his jaw. The others strained to hear something other than the whisper of tree limbs in the breeze. There it was for a second. Then gone. And then again; a sort of melodious purring. The wind caught the noise this time, bringing it to them briefly.

"That's the sound of wings!" Carl yelled. He jumped up and raced outside; Camille and Jack followed a little slower. Maria joined them as they gathered outside the shelter.

"Headed this way!" Carl announced with rising urgency.

"Down to the airstrip!" Jack called, hobbling along on one-and-a-half legs.

"Where is it? Where is it?" Maria cried. "Are they coming for us?"

They broke out of the trees and scanned the skies above, searching the floating patches of blue and grey for a pinhead speck. Strange little spots danced before their unblinking eyes in the eternity of seconds it took for them to locate the plane.

"There she is!" Jack announced, pointing triumphantly skyward. Just a black dot above the tree line, the plane buzzed closer until the others could see it too.

"What is it?" Maria wanted to know. "Are they coming for us?"

"It *could* be a search . . ." Carl said hopefully.

"Too early," Jack cautioned.

"We need to signal! Flares or a flag, or something!" cried Carl.

Wordless, Camille passed Carl her compact. He fiddled it open with nervous fingers, spilling powder all over himself, and flashed the mirror toward the sun. The little group watched breathlessly as the small plane winged over the treetops, growing bigger each second.

"Cessna 140," said Carl, still working the mirror. "It's a two-seater."

"And headed for the hangar," Jack added dolefully.

"No, they've seen us!" Carl countered, flashing the mirror wildly. "They're going to come about!"

"They're avoiding that cloud bank, Carl."

"No, they've seen us!" Carl sputtered angrily. "They have to!"

"All they can see is that approaching storm. They probably think your signal is lightning."

Carl turned on Jack vehemently. "It doesn't look anything like lightning!"

"Well, it might if you were them and you had *that* on your tail." Jack waved at the glowering storm approaching; dark thunderheads rising rapidly, the first few drops starting to fall as the wind picked up.

Carl stared at the disappearing Cessna in disbelief. "No," he muttered, shaking his head. "No, you can't leave us here. Come back!" He waved his arm in a broad arc, knowing full well that it was useless. The airplane flashed once more in the light and was gone. Carl staggered down the airstrip in the direction it had been traveling, the mirrored compact still clamped in his hand. "Why didn't you see us?" He directed his question to the clouds. "And if you did see us, why didn't you show us? At least give us some hope?"

"Carl. Come on. Back to the shelter before we're all soaked." It was practical Jack. He and Maria were on their way to the dugout already.

Carl turned. Camille was standing stock-still and ashen faced, looking off into the building clouds.

"Come on, Camille," Carl urged gently. "Let's get under shelter before this storm breaks."

Tears filled her eyes as she pointed to her compact in his hand. "Did that scare them off?"

Carl shook his head. "No, Jack's right. With a storm like this, you can't stay up in a little plane. If they did, they'd soon be in the same boat we are. Hey, it's starting to pour! We'd better make a run for it!"

Carl grabbed Camille's arm and propelled her up the hill ahead of him as rain dissolved the slope into a gooey, sticky slide. They soon caught up with Jack, thanks to Carl's manpower, and the girls were sent on ahead while Carl helped him up the hill. They fell only once, Jack sliding several feet, griming the front of his suit in red clay.

Carl knelt beside him, his back soaked already. "Come on, Jack, you've gotta get up."

Panting from his efforts, Jack nodded. "Yeah, you go on ahead. I'll be up in a minute."

"You get up now, Jack. Look, you've got only thirty feet to go." Carl waved at the hovel just as Camille and Maria stepped out. "Get back inside!" he yelled.

Camille made a trumpet with her hands. "Where's Eddy?"

"What?"

"Eddy's gone!"

Several quick steps brought Carl to the dugout entrance. "Impossible! He can't be—"

"He is, Carl. I looked. He's not in there."

Carl's stomach knotted. "Well, he can't have gone far," he said, knowing full well that Eddy could—and in his current condition, most likely would. He glanced at Jack, who had pulled himself up the slope on his belly: dragging one leg, pushing with the other.

"Go. I'll be fine."

"Right."

"We're coming too!" said Maria.

"No," Carl started, then checked. He directed a quick, questioning look at Jack, who nodded in answer.

"Okay," Carl nodded to Camille and Maria. "But you two stay in constant contact—understand? Constant contact! If you need anything, holler!"

"Carl."

"What?" He looked back in time to catch the .45 that Jack flung at him. "Thanks," he said, and tromped off into the brush to find Eddy Martin. Again.

CHAPTER NINE

ONE SMALL SEED

The shoe had to go. It was too tight: cutting off circulation, smothering his toes. With a morbid sense of curiosity as to whether it was all that held his foot together, Jack leaned forward to untie it. He couldn't reach. Now he knew he was not as young, or as limber, as he once was, but really! This was ridiculous! It had to be the way his leg was splinted. *All right, fine.* He drew up his right foot, removed the shoe and sock, and used his toes to free the other foot. The toes of his left foot had a ghostly bluish cast. Very unnatural to his warm, brown skin. And swollen—was it ever! He loosened his tie . . . the one that held a sappy pine branch to his leg.

The Spam was sizzling in its can; the broth water was hot. When would the others return for breakfast? It had been nearly forty minutes since the incessant calls for

Eddy had grown faint and faded into the distance. He would give them another five before ditching breakfast plans and going after them.

"Hello, Jack."

He looked up, startled. "Why, hello," he said, regaining his mental equilibrium.

"Where is everybody?"

"Out looking for you."

"For *me?*" Eddy frowned, and scratched a bit of crusted blood from his forehead. "Well," he shrugged finally, "I'm right here."

"So I see," said Jack. The task now would be to keep him here. "You didn't happen to run into anyone else?"

"No, I didn't see them," said Eddy, brushing raindrops from his lightly dampened hair.

"That's too bad," said Jack. "How about some breakfast?"

"Breakfast?" Eddy wrinkled his nose slightly and looked disdainfully at the Spam. "Nah. I just ate."

"Really? What'd you have?"

"Eggs. Toast. Blackberry preserves. The eggs were a bit greasy," he admitted. "And the toast was a little dark. But on the whole . . ." He glared again at the Spam and raised one eyebrow. "I was expecting you all to join me up at the cabin," Eddy continued with a jerk of his thumb. "I'll bet this roof leaks pretty bad."

"It does," Jack nodded. "Oh, by the way, Eddy, where is this cabin?"

An expression of innocent surprise wrote itself across Eddy's face. "Well, don't you remember, Jack? It's just north, er . . . east of here about three miles," he replied. He was pointing southwest.

"No, I don't remember. Why would I?"

Eddy raised his eyebrows. "Because you slept there last night! Boy, Jack, I don't know about you!"

"Oh yes, of course. *That* cabin."

"Well yeah, that cabin. What cabin did you think I meant? Anyway," he shrugged, "I'm gonna go check my snares. I'm thinking I've got at least one hare. Maybe a couple—"

"Wait! Eddy." Jack couldn't let him get away now. "Do you think you could check my leg for me?"

"Check your leg?" Eddy knelt down beside Jack and examined the splinted limb. "Boy, what'd you do to yourself?"

"Oh, I took a fall," said Jack.

"Must have been quite a fall," laughed Eddy. "Nice splint job, by the way—but it's too tight now." Eddy loosened the bandages. "I wish Pops could see me now! It might make up for me dropping out of med school."

"I wish your pop could see you, too, Eddy. As a matter of fact," said Jack, "I wish he could see all of us."

Doctor Robert Martin, a surgeon well known in England and America before the war, had earned greater recognition during and after, for his success in treating battle-torn soldiers.

"You know, Jack, I think you'd better put your foot up and give the swelling a chance to go down."

"Well all right. I will—if you'll tend the fire and keep the food from burning."

Eddy took a moment to weigh his options. His snares needed to be checked and he was obviously anxious to retrieve his catch before it was stolen or went to waste. But Jack's leg looked pretty bad; it really needed some care. "Okay," he said after a bit. Duty and his doctoring instinct had won out. "Lie down and I'll raise your leg up above your heart." He grabbed Camille's suitcase and a bundle of clothes to prop up the leg. "Can you wiggle your toes?"

"At the moment, I can't even feel my toes, and that's a mercy."

"I'll bet it is." Eddy paused in his ministrations as Carl and the girls ducked through the doorway. "Just look what the dog brought in!" he called cheerfully.

Carl sank to the floor, looking rather too close to Eddy's description of him. His glare at Eddy was almost unfriendly.

"What made you come out of hiding, Eddy?"

"Hiding? I was just up at the cabin."

At the sight of her husband, Maria rushed to embrace him. "Eddy! You gave us such a fright!"

He stiffened and pulled back, blushing to the roots of his hair. "Oh. Did I?"

"Ed—" Maria began, then she too checked, and gasped; the realization coming like a plunge of frigid water.

"Steady, girl," Jack warned.

Maria swallowed hard. "Camille sprained her ankle," she said, forcing her voice against a tremor. "Do you think you could look at it?"

Eddy chuckled, and nodded at Jack. "First him, now you; anyone would think I was a doctor!"

"Not quite, but good in a pinch," said Jack.

"I wish Pops could see me now!" crowed Eddy.

"So do I," Carl nodded miserably. "So do we all!"

❧ ❧ ❧

"Will you have a drink, Mr. Jensen?"

Harry's stomach turned a somersault at the mention of it. He would have thought, for a man of such wealth and influence, that Milford Smith would have decent taste in liquors. Such was not the case. For his part, he would prefer to spend a month on navy coffee.

"We can dispense with the formal niceties, Mr. Smith," said Harry. "What I have to say is far too important for that."

"Impossible!" Milford cracked a smile and poured himself a glass of cherry-red liquor. "You are certain you don't care to join me?"

"I am." Harry stood up, releasing any further doubt from Milford's mind. "Your aircraft is missing," he said simply.

Milford took a long sip and smiled. "Now what do you mean by that?"

"Your aircraft is missing!" Harry repeated the phrase slowly and distinctly. "Is there anything difficult to understand about that?"

"What makes you say that?"

Harry sat down again. "My boys missed their meeting with Cal Beckett early this afternoon."

The fat man laughed between sips. "I can well believe that. Turn them loose in California and they are bound to have a little fun. And with the way you drive them, I should think they needed a vacation. Think of it: warm, sunny California—things to do, places to go, people to meet. They're bound to go a little crazy."

"Yes," Harry responded dryly. "And of all those people to meet, Cal Beckett was the most important. I know my boys, Smith, and I know this is not their MO. Now, I can't say whether this is some of your funny work or what; but let me tell you, I intend to get to the bottom of it if I have to call in the army and navy along with the police department."

He finally had Milford's attention. "Now wait a minute, Jensen, let's not be too hasty. We have no proof of anything going afoul."

"No, we don't," Harry admitted. "Just a hunch. But that's still good enough for me to go and alert the entire—"

"Please! Have a drink, Harry. Your nerves are shot. Ugh! You're sick with fever and should be in bed!"

"Maybe that's true," Harry answered. "But now let me tell you something that will wreck your nerves, Milford."

He leaned forward in the overstuffed chair. "I know *you*, Milford. I know enough to bust you wide open."

"I wouldn't advise that, Harry," Milford cautioned with a cold determination in his voice.

"No, of course not. But I can. And I will. I happen to feel a fatherly responsibility for those boys of mine—and if you've pulled a fast one on them, I'll—"

"No, no! Harry, please!" Milford was again conciliatory. "You forget that my own boy was piloting that plane. The only child of my only son . . ."

"No, I didn't forget that: because I also happen to know you are a man of very few scruples. You may like the kid, but you like your money more."

"You really think I'm heartless!" Milford declared.

"No, I don't: I know it."

"Harry, friend, you jump to such conclusions. Even if I did want to be rid of the boy, do you think I would crash my own plane? I don't have to tell you that craft cost a pretty penny, even for me! Oh come on, man, have a drink to settle your nerves and we'll talk more about it. There is certainly a simple explanation!"

❧ ❧ ❧

"So," Carl sighed. "What's all this? About a cabin?" He glanced furtively at the three in the corner: Maria assisting Eddy as he cut bandages and wrapped Camille's ankle.

"I don't know," said Jack. He tossed one of Camille's peppermints to Carl and popped another in his own mouth.

Carl stared at the cheerful, striped candy in his palm, then his fingers closed over it. "What do you think, a return to Boy Scout years? He's really lost it, Jack. He needs to be in bed. Do you think we can keep him—"

"You think he's lost it?"

"Uh, Jack, when a fellow doesn't recognize his own wife, it seems pretty clear—"

"But the cabin—you don't believe him?"

"No," Carl said flatly. "He's given me every reason *not* to believe him. The poor guy just needs help."

Jack nodded his assent. "So what do you say we do?"

"You? Put him to bed and sit tight."

Jack grunted. "And what will you be doing meantime?"

Carl was slow in responding. "You see that mountain over there?" He nodded over Jack's shoulder.

"I've noticed it a time or two," Jack remarked without turning. "But I don't think so. At any rate, you're in no shape to try."

Carl's voice had a newly whetted edge. "And d'you think we'll be in any better shape if I don't?"

Jack shrugged. "Maybe. Maybe not. There'll be a search. I expect it will be thorough."

"There's a lot of territory between Colorado and California. Are you counting on them being on time?"

"I guess you know *I'm* not," said Jack. "But for the others . . . There's always Eddy's cabin."

Carl groaned.

"And here I thought you liked hiking," Jack returned with a smile.

"Don't be crazy, Jack! There's no point in letting him goose-chase all over this mudslide! It's a waste of valuable energy."

"Hmm. I think he'll find it."

"You do?" Carl's voice rose in pitch. "W-w-what makes you say that?"

"Well, I was thinking." Jack closed his eyes and sucked his cheeks in, relishing the sweet-cold spice of peppermint that still lingered in his mouth. "When you got back in here you were pretty much soaked through—still are plenty wet: better turn and let the fire warm your backside. Eddy was dry."

"So he found a thick tree and sat under it," said Carl, turning round. "That doesn't—"

"Reason number two," cut in Jack. "When he came back he was talking about breakfast: eggs and toast and blackberry preserves."

"Yeah, so?"

"He had a blackberry seed stuck in his teeth."

Carl shrugged one shoulder. "Who's to say he didn't find some berries—"

"Reason number three: if there *is* a cabin three miles from here, and Eddy's found it, how'd you like to die of exposure because we didn't believe him?"

Carl opened his hand and stared at the candy as if he did not know how it had come to be there. "I told you what I think," he said slowly.

Jack nodded. "And I said 'no.' All feelings aside, Carl, you're of more value dying here with us than playing the hero's part and dying on that mountain."

One corner of Carl's nose lifted. "Is that . . . an order, then?"

Jack's voice warmed. "No. No, Carl, it isn't that. It's a suggestion. More—a request. From a friend."

With a sudden moan, Carl dropped his forehead to his hand.

"Come on, Carl. Tie a knot and hang on. You stayed six months behind the line when you said you couldn't go another minute."

"That's not counting the time in the Gestapo hole," Carl said, his voice rasping.

"There. Seven and a half months. And why'd you do it, Carl? To save the lives of a bunch of guys you've never met. Well, now you can do the same for your friends. I'm not asking you for six months, Carl. I'm only asking for a week; or maybe a little more if there's any of us out here still kicking. One week. You can do that, Carl."

"Right now, Jack, I can't—I can hardly hold my head up . . ."

"Sure. You've taken it on the chin for all of us. So go knock off for a bit. I'll watch things here. And then we'll see about Eddy's cabin."

CHAPTER TEN

A BATHTUB FULL OF HOLES

The needle on the fuel gauge wavered dangerously near empty. Nick leaned toward the left side of the cockpit to offer his older cousin a friendly suggestion.

"Um, don't you think it's time to switch to the other tank?"

Frank snapped back like a taut rubber band. "This *is* the other tank, Nick!"

"Oh. That's too bad." Nick had a reputation for understatement. Turning to look out the window, he watched the sea of trees below. Seemingly endless trees. An involuntary shudder ran down the length of his spine at the thought of ditching here. But that was not the only thought that bothered him. His mind traced the events of the morning: the conversation with his father that had become so heated, and ended in his storming out of the house.

"Don't go flying with Frank!" his father had called after him. "He'll kill you both!"

Now why hadn't he listened? Why had he been so impatient? Uncle George had promised to take him up today. Couldn't he have waited another two hours? Then he would be in the much-preferable position of being on the ground wishing to fly instead of flying and wishing he was safe on the ground.

It had been a beautiful day to fly, though. Too beautiful, in fact. They had lost track of time—and a few other things—and the storm had come upon them out of nowhere.

"I don't suppose you happen to know of an airstrip nearby," Nick asked hopefully.

"No!" Frank growled. "Maybe you'd like to step out and take a look?"

"No thanks," Nick sighed. "Do you think we have enough fuel to make it back?"

"Look, if you think I'm not doing my job—"

A sudden flash of light caught Nick's eye. "Hey, what was that?"

"What was what?" Frank responded sourly.

"I saw . . . say, that looks like an airstrip!"

"That's no airstrip, Nick!" Frank growled between clenched teeth.

"Yes it is! And there's an air—" Or was it? Some twisted pieces of metal. A scorched patch on the ground.

Was this the site of a forced landing? Was that an airplane's smoldering carcass? What of the pilot? Passengers?

The light flashed again.

"I say! Frank, there's a bunch of people down there!" Nick pressed his nose against the window, straining to get a better view. "Turn around; I think they're trying to signal!"

Frank set his teeth and stared straight ahead, not altering course one iota. "There's no one down there, Nick!"

"Yes there is, and they're signaling."

"That's lightning."

"It is not!" Nick cried indignantly. He might not know about flying, but he could tell lightning when he saw it. "There are people down there, Frank. And I think they need help."

"So do we," snarled Frank.

They were past the airstrip now. Nick turned in his seat to get one last look. "But if they've crashed and are stranded—they might *die*, Frank."

"If you want to help," said Frank, "I'll let you out here."

Nick bit his lip, noting the sincerity in Frank's voice. It *would* lighten the load. He checked the fuel gauge again and shrugged. Perhaps he would be joining them soon enough.

❧ ❧ ❧

"Yessir, two airplanes," Ferguson nodded. "Twin sisters, custom built for Mr. Smith by Jensen's Manufacturing. I maintained 'em both."

"And they were both scheduled to fly that day?" Inspector Rigby leaned back in his chair and wove a pencil between his fingers.

"Yeah, the both of 'em. One by Smith's grandson, Walter Westman. He was headed to California with a load of people from Jensen's. There was a fella in California who was interested in the custom Bonanza, so Mr. Jensen, being a bit chummy with Mr. Smith, worked out an agreement to borrow the plane for the weekend."

"Uh-huh. And the other?"

"There was a couple o' guys—foreigners. Don't know their business, or where they were going. I just maintain the planes!" Ferguson objected, raising his hands defensively.

"Right," the inspector said slowly. "Continue."

"Well, for the one, 71Tango, Mr. Smith required, er . . . *special* maintenance."

"What do you mean, *special?*"

"Just special. It's not something you do every day, you know. But I was just following orders! I didn't mean nothing by it! I was just following my orders!"

ɛ𝔬 ɞ ɛ𝔬

Eddy sat up slowly, eyes deeply expressive of pain. "Huh? What's that?" he asked, bleary with sleep.

"I said we're moving to the cabin," said Carl. "There's another storm blowing in and this old bungalow leaks like your mother's colander!"

"Oh. That's okay. I'll wait here 'til you get back."

"No, Eddy, we need your help." It was Jack. His smooth talking had often brought Eddy around to their point of view: he made unashamed use of it now. "Carl's forgotten the way already."

"Right: use me as the scapegoat," Carl muttered.

Eddy appealed to Jack's horse sense. "But Jack, you remember. Don't you?"

"Well, no. I'm a bit sketchy myself."

"Then how am I . . . ? You fellas know I'm terrible with directions."

"Come on, Ed. You said it was about three miles north, er . . . east of here." Jack was pointing southwest.

Eddy looked at him, puzzled. "You're confused," he said finally, shaking his head.

Jack nodded. "Yes, that's why we need your help." He knew he had won then. Eddy shrugged and dragged himself to his feet, still half asleep.

"Which way did you say it was?"

"North, er . . . east." This time it was Carl who repeated the dysfunctional formula.

"No, that can't be right!" Eddy insisted. "That's not east." His left arm shot out full length. "*This* is east!"

Carl's jaw went slack. Even Jack managed to look faintly surprised. Eddy was dead on. "What?" Eddy asked with a twitch of his eyebrows. "This *is* east, isn't it?"

Carl nodded slowly.

"Yes, Eddy," Jack agreed.

"Well then," Eddy shrugged. Problem solved. Now he would go back to bed.

"That didn't work too well," Carl whispered to Jack.

Jack scratched behind his ear. "No," he agreed.

"So now what?"

"Plan B."

"What's Plan B?"

Jack shook his head. "Don't know yet." To Eddy he said, "Somehow that doesn't seem quite right. The directions must have gotten scrambled. Let's see you fly by the seat of your pants, Eddy. We've got to get to that cabin before the storm hits: Carl can't stand another soaking."

"There you go again," Carl murmured out one side of his mouth.

"Shut up and like it," Jack replied in kind.

Eddy looked with genuine concern at Carl, who for Eddy's benefit, did his best impression of being cold and miserable. He was.

"All right, let's go," Eddy said. He stepped out of their dugout and hid his eyes from the sudden, blinding light. Several minutes passed. He lowered his arms cautiously, swayed a little on his feet, and proceeded forward.

ꕤ ꕤ ꕤ

"Holes in the oilpan?"

The mechanic nodded. "Seven of 'em."

A low whistle. "And you filled them with wax?"

Another nod.

"And then as the engine heated up, the wax . . . Yikes." Rigby scratched his head. "Sort of like a . . . a . . ."

"Bathtub full of holes," Ferguson put in dully.

CHAPTER ELEVEN

CABIN, CABIN

"I'd like to file a missing persons report!"

The clerk behind the counter hardly opened her eyes. Clearly, five cups of coffee were not enough for one day. "Name?"

"Camille Jensen, Jack SuLong, Edward Martin, Carl Linder, Walter Westman."

This time the clerk lifted her eyes, pen hovering over a long form. "*Your* name?" Her tone was ice.

Harry leaned his elbows on the counter. "Look, sister, I want to talk with someone about this. So if you'll toddle off and find them, it will at least spare you the paperwork!"

From down the hallway came a voice, addressing no one in particular. "Like a bathtub full of holes! Of course, of course! A bathtub full of holes! Now why didn't I think of that?"

Soon a body followed the voice, wearing a bulky overcoat and crumpled fedora. It brushed past Harry, coffee in one hand as it waved at the clerk with the other. "Goodnight Gina, Leslie, whichever you are."

"Goodnight, Inspector," the clerk replied. "Don't forget to write!" She turned to Harry again. "*Your* name?"

"Hold that thought, Gina or Leslie," answered Harry. He bolted out the door of the police station as a car pulled abruptly from the curb. The inspector's face was contorted and red as he exclaimed at his driver from behind the windshield glass. Fresh hot coffee was dripping down his front.

"Now if I know anything . . ." Harry mused. He nodded, hopped in his car, and pulled into traffic. If he knew anything, Inspector Rigby was headed for the Smith residence.

ꟷ ꟷ ꟷ

Camille did not like the idea. Not one little bit. Eddy should be kept in bed and closely monitored. Jack should keep his leg elevated. And Carl . . . well there wasn't much that could be done for him until help arrived. But to go hiking in his condition was the height of insanity. As for herself—she would manage somehow.

Her face twitched slightly at the weight of another step. The handle of Westman's duffle cut into her palm. A glance back showed Maria pulling with both hands on Camille's bag, dragging it forward. Sighing, Camille slung Westman's duffle over her shoulder. Manning her crutch with one hand, she offered the other to Maria.

"No, it's okay. I can get it," said Maria, readjusting her grip. A few minutes more and she dropped the bag to her side. "I thought they said only three miles."

Camille stopped to catch her breath, looking at the hobbling figure of Jack a hundred feet farther along on the path. Carl and Eddy were only noises—bushes and twigs crunching and snapping as they cut through the scrubby overgrowth toward what they hoped would be a cabin. Every now and then Carl's voice wafted back to her, exclamatory, exasperated. "Eddy! Eddy, hold up a bit!"

"I think we've gone only two and a half," Camille answered Maria honestly.

"We can't keep pace with them. We should have weighted Eddy down with the bags," said Maria.

Camille shrugged. "Too late for that now."

"Oh well," said Maria. "Let's just keep going and do the best we can."

"You go along ahead—I'll be with you in a bit."

"Well, all right. But don't be too long."

"I won't." Camille leaned against a boulder and unfastened the buckles on her brace. Just as she thought: blisters. The beginnings of blisters, at least. Her brace had been rubbing for the past several weeks. Her appointment to get fitted with a new one was on Tuesday. That wouldn't help her much now. She would try a little padding once they reached the cabin. *If* they reached the cabin. But now she needed to hurry along or be left behind.

Maria's voice called back to her. "Camille! Are you coming?"

"Yes, I'm coming." Camille fumbled with the buckles.

Maria looked back to check on her and screamed.

ꕤ ꕤ ꕤ

Eddy was beginning to slacken his madman's pace. Not because he was tired. Not him. A fidgety uneasiness as he stopped, looked about, continued, and stopped again, told Carl what it meant: Eddy was lost.

Carl sucked air slowly between his teeth as he turned sideways to wait for Jack. "I think our hound has lost the scent," he informed Jack at his approach.

Jack was puffing for breath. "It rather looks that way," he nodded.

"Do we call him off now?"

"No, not yet. But I don't like to be so strung out. You go ahead, try to keep him reined in. I'll drop back and bring up the rear."

"Right. Trying to keep up with this nut is like gargling with peanut butter!"

Just then Eddy emerged from the brush to Carl's right. He wrenched out a dead branch that barred his path, flung it over his shoulder, and stomped over to them, fairly drooping. "It's no use." He shook his head. "I don't remember. I can't find it. Sorry Carl, I just can't find it."

"That's okay, Eddy," Carl shrugged. He was more concerned that his friend would work himself into a fit than the fact that he could not find a cabin, the very existence of which he still doubted.

Eddy was not so easily consoled. "I'm sorry, Jack," he continued. "I tried, but everything looks different. Can't seem to get my bearings . . . Everything looks funny." He was shaking his head, rubbing his eyes, his agitation growing by the second. Jack and Carl looked at each other in alarm.

Then a shrill noise rang through the air. Eddy jerked like he was touching a live wire. Without a word, he turned back down their path and charged through the brush.

ꟃ ꟃ ꟃ

At first Camille thought Maria had been bitten by something, for the violent shriek she gave. She looked up quickly, half fearing Maria was at that moment being torn to pieces. But there she was, in no apparent danger. Why then was she still screaming?

Slowly, Camille turned her head, and the cause of Maria's outburst turned her to stone. A tawny body crouched but thirty feet from her, four paws and a tail, eyes gleaming evil yellow. Caught in the entrancing stare, Camille could not draw a breath, much less give voice to terror. The cougar flicked a taunting tail, creeping forward on a prey that never tried to run; it stopped and calculated for a spring, shifting weight in its hind end like a batter awaiting the first pitch.

Maria flung into Camille, knocking her to the side; her arm hurled a stone at the cat, but with poor trajectory.

Ears flattened. The cat raised its lips to snarl at the insult. More projectiles followed. Maria employed everything in reach: sticks, stones, Westman's duffle. But more effective, the fearsome hysteria of noise.

"Out! Get back! Run! *Eddy!*"

This last was answered in a barrage, a rush. Instead of a pounce, a yelp, as the cat found itself attacked by Eddy and a stout tree branch. Unable to fathom such an onslaught, the cougar backed away from the grievous blows, pausing just once to lash back with its paw. Eddy gave the animal no chance for thought, not a second's respite from the beatings until it turned full tail and fled.

Time seemed to pass Camille in a hushed blur of commotion. Carl, suddenly beside her, bid her speak. She felt his grip on her arm, so tight it was painful. But was that arm really hers?

Maria was embracing Eddy. They spoke excitedly, laughed, all very loud and animated. All Camille heard was the humming of blood in her ears.

Carl shook her. "Camille, for the last time, are you all right?"

She nodded and fell against his shoulder with a dry sob. Carl put an arm around her, and began to chuckle. "You know, Eddy, you looked crazy going after that cat! Boy, I'll never forget the look on pussy's face. Okay," he said, sobering up. "Maybe it's not time to laugh yet, but give it a couple years and this is bound to be funny."

"I'll laugh with you in two years." Eddy clamped a hand over the scratch in his forearm. "It was a young cat, Carl. They stay with their mums for two years or so."

Carl dug around in Westman's duffle for a shirt to stanch Eddy's blood.

"If he's gone off to squeal on me," Eddy looked at Carl, "then when he comes back, *you* can take the missus!"

"Sure. With one arm." Carl looked around uneasily. "Why don't we move along now?"

"Good idea. Where are we going?" Eddy asked.

"Hey! What's all the excitement here?" Jack asked, hobbling down the trail to join them.

"Oh, Eddy's just harassing the wildlife," Carl answered flippantly.

Jack eyed Eddy's bleeding arm. "That would explain the unholy yowling I heard."

"Yeah," Carl snickered. "It was Eddy. Say, where were you and Mr. Wesson when we needed you?"

Jack answered in perfect deadpan. "Mr. Wesson and I sat down quickly when wooden leg stolen from under us." He bowed to Eddy. "Humble tailbone thanks you."

"Oh. Sorry, Jack," Eddy apologized. "I didn't mean to knock you over: guess I didn't really see you there. Just like I didn't really see that kitty 'til after the second swipe I took at him." He kicked at Jack's branch. "I sort of busted your crutch."

"That's okay. I've found a new one. Shall we continue to the cabin now?"

"Yes, let's!" The words were in unison from three mouths.

Eddy looked blank. "Cabin? What cabin? Have you been here before, Jack? Carl?"

"Oh no!" Carl moaned. "Boy Scout's gone."

"You don't remember, Eddy? You had breakfast there this morning."

"What? I did not!"

"Eggs and toast with blackberry preserves," said Jack.

"I don't know what you guys are talking about: I've never been here before in my life!" He looked around. Everyone was watching him, half disappointed, half expectant. "Hey! What is this? I don't get it!"

Maria's eyes sought his. "Eddy, are you *sure* you don't remember a cabin?"

He stared back in bewilderment. "Maria, would I *lie?*"

"Never mind, Eddy," said Jack. "Well, boys and girls, it looks like we're going back to the dugout. About face!"

Camille groaned inwardly. They had trekked all this way for nothing. She sat a minute longer, trying to find strength to stand on legs that felt like spaghetti. "This won't be forever." The words sounded in her head. They had buoyed her lagging spirits many a time before. When things were too hard to bear and then got worse, those words comforted her. "This won't be forever." The words her brave captain spoke before marching off . . . forever. They echoed the sentiment her mother had taught from Scripture: It came to pass. Not to stay.

Carl reached down to help her up. Yes, her legs would hold her weight. Yes, she could stand. Camille smiled weakly up at him.

"You gonna be okay?"

She nodded. "I'll be—" The final word did not come. Her mouth hung open, and she stared.

Carl turned his head slowly. His hair prickled on the back of his neck. Then he too just stared. "Hey . . ." he said finally, and pointed.

The others looked in the direction indicated. And there it was as Eddy had said. About three miles north . . . er, east . . . er, southwest of the dugout, up the slope and concealed by a tangle of trees. A soft moss-covered roof. A brick chimney still smoking. Eddy's cabin.

And was that the smell of eggs and toast cooking?

CHAPTER TWELVE

PULLING RANK

Maria breathed a ragged sigh as Carl tugged the sagging, squeaking door shut. Safety. For a moment, that was enough. Then, as her eyes adjusted to the dimness, she did not see the cobwebs, the grand, ancestral home of untold spider generations. Nor did she notice the dirt that scuffed beneath their feet, or the dust carpeting the corners of the room. Instead, she was impressed by the wondrous, palatial quality of the place, for there, running parallel to the far wall—beds! A set of bunks, the lower a double size. Beds and blankets to go with them.

There were pantry shelves well-stocked: Spam, canned green beans and pears, bags of dry beans and somewhat buggy flour, powdered milk, a small stash of chocolate—real chocolate. Why, here was food to last them a month!

There was a tin of medical supplies: gauze and bandages for Camille's blisters, antibiotic ointment and dressings for Eddy's arm. An old wooden trunk stood near the pantry shelves containing several articles of surplus Forest Service clothing: woolen socks, trousers and sweaters; too long or too wide to fit any of them properly, but welcome just the same.

Maria beamed at Eddy. "It's wonderful, Ed."

Jack nodded and slapped Eddy on the back. "You done good, ol' boy."

Eddy just shook his head and shrugged. "Oh, Carl's the one who spotted it," he said.

"Actually, Camille gets credit for that," said Carl.

All eyes turned to Camille, who, sitting on the lower bunk, had just removed her brace, exposing an atrophied and deformed calf with an ugly case of blisters. Her cheeks bloomed red and she quickly tucked the leg under her skirt.

"It doesn't matter who saw it first," said Jack, sensitive to Camille's embarrassment. "What matters is that it's found and we make proper use of—"

Carl interrupted with a sharp exclamation and started for the corner near the door. Jack saw it too, and threw himself forward, blocking Carl's path with his crutch, though that pretty maneuver nearly landed him on his face.

"No, don't touch it: I saw it first!"

"You just got done saying it didn't matter who saw it first," Carl objected, trying to knock the crutch away.

"Don't touch it," Jack repeated. He pulled a chair up to the table that held a confusion of knobs and wires:

an ancient and very filthy FM radio. "Go find something else to do before you mess it all up. Leave this baby to me!"

Carl grunted in disappointment and left Jack to work his wonders. He noted a pint jar of preserves on the table, two-thirds gone, and picked it up, hiding it in his hand. "Hey Eddy, what kind?"

"How should I know?" Eddy asked through gritted teeth.

"Well, guess."

"If you'll forgive me," he held up his bleeding arm. "I have other, more pressing matters at hand."

"Right," Carl grimaced. He moved across the room to Camille. "How're you doing?" he asked.

"I'm fine," she said with face averted.

He studied her profile. Her eyes seemed sunken, her skin drawn tight like a drumhead. Had she slept at all last night? Or even for the past week? Her Uncle Harry overworked her. And Camille herself did not know how to stop.

The wrinkles stacked up on Carl's forehead. "Camille, I think you'd better go to bed. We'll tend your blisters later. Better have an aspirin," he added.

"I don't want an aspirin," Camille murmured.

"I said you'd better have one."

"Carl!" The sudden, sharp exclamation brought all eyes in the cabin to her. It was the closest most had ever come to hearing her raise her voice. "I don't want an aspirin! I just want to go home!" Grabbing a blanket, she pulled it tight around her shoulders and rolled into bed.

Carl paused, the white medicine bottle in hand. *I just want to go home.* It was an odd concept for him. Of course, he had no one to go home to. His biological father had abandoned his mother months before he came along. And she, forced to move on with the other migratory farm workers, had left him at a children's hospital as a three-year-old, doubtless expecting he would die from the pneumonia that filled his lungs. Adopted by the elderly Mr. and Mrs. Linder, he was seventeen when they both died, and he was on his own. There was no one else. Never had been. Now, probably never would be. This was just another part of life. Inconvenient, for sure. Uncomfortable, yes indeed. Certainly not what he would have planned for himself. But the company, he had to admit, was not half bad. In fact, it could not be better. If he must be stranded, let it be with his best friends, while his boss headed up a search for them.

So what was this about Camille wanting to go home? Home to what? To whom? To a drunken and abusive, albeit paralyzed, father? Or to a tired and weary stepmother who spent her days placating the former? Or was it her war-crippled, embittered brother, lone survivor of the seven, that Camille wished for?

Perhaps by "home" she meant the house of her Uncle Harry, where she had lived off and on through the years. But even there, though she was loved as a daughter, she was worked as a slave. What was this mysterious concept of "home" she spoke of?

Maria sank to the bed beside Camille and caressed her back. "Camille dear, it will be okay!"

Camille lashed out angrily: "Of course it will be okay! It's always okay! Everybody always says so—but that never changes anything!" She smothered her face against the lumpy mattress, her last words lost in strangled sobs.

Maria sat by her until the noise quieted and died back to a muted weeping. Only then did she turn to Carl, who looked on in perplexed helplessness. "She's tired," Maria said softly. "The fright of the cat—Just give her some time."

Carl nodded.

"And now," Maria rose, rolling up her sleeves. "First things first. Hot water and bandages." She moved to the fireplace.

"Need some help with that?" Carl asked.

Maria laughed. "My daddy led the Scouts for twenty-five years—I *think* I picked up on how to start a fire in that time! But if you could lend Eddy a hand . . ."

Her husband had his medical kit spread on the table and was dabbing at his arm with an alcohol-soaked swab.

"Need some help there, Eddy?"

"Sure," he said, surrendering the swab to Carl. Then almost immediately: "Oh ouch! Take it easy, Carl! That *is* my arm—and it's still attached!"

"Sorry," said Carl, remembering too late to be gentle. "I thought it was *filet d'Eddy.*"

"That's not barbecue sauce you've got there." Eddy winced again. "I think I could do a better job with my foot!"

"You still have one hand—maybe you should use it."

"I would—but it's a clumsy left hand."

"Yeah, well mine's a clumsy right."

"Forgot about that, Lefty." Eddy took a fresh swab and finished cleaning any area that wasn't already stinging. Presently, Maria brought a pot of boiling water to the table, a tangle of fishing line bubbling inside.

"He ordered the spaghetti," said Carl. "I'm having the beefsteak. And could you remind the cook to keep it just a gentle medium-rare with plenty of onions and horseradish?"

"I'm sorry," Maria said, "but we're just out of beefsteak." Her voice sounded odd. White knuckles gripped the back of Eddy's chair. Carl jumped up to steady her if necessary.

"No, I'm fine," she told him, drawing a deep breath.

"I warned you not to look, Maria," said Eddy.

"I thought maybe I'd gotten over it," said Maria, retreating to her kitchen.

Eddy slapped his last swab down on the table. "Well, I never thought I'd be telling this one on myself." He paused to take some fishing line from the hot water bath. "Know why I dropped out of med school?"

"What's this?" Carl grinned. "A deep, dark secret that survived the war? Thought I'd heard 'em all!"

"I was working as an intern in the ER the summer of my second year," Eddy explained. "And we saw everything. All the blood and guts you could ever want: automobile accidents, policemen getting gunned down, did my first emergency appendectomy, and the usual handful of broken bones and whatnot. It was great: firsthand experience, and I was really enjoying it. Then little Johnny Hansen comes in with his mum, howling and carrying on about his finger that he's sliced open with his pocket knife."

"Yeah, just like I'm gonna be doing here in a minute," said Carl as he watched Eddy thread a needle.

"You'd better not be!" Eddy warned. He went on with his story. "Well, I'd known the kid since he was born; he lived across the street from me for several years. So when Johnny realized he was all set to get stitched up, he tried changing his tune, saying it really wasn't so bad: nothing a chocolate malt wouldn't fix. No dice. He had bone showing, blood going everywhere—"

"Please!" begged Carl. "I've got a weak stomach!"

Eddy was unsympathetic. "He was gonna get stitches. So I stuck a needle in to numb it and he let out a scream like an Indian war whoop. Next thing I knew, I was picking myself up off the floor. And I turned and walked out of there and never looked back: ended my medical career right there. Called Pops to tell him I wanted nothing to do with anything that screams or bleeds."

"Right," Carl snickered and looked up from Eddy's arm to glance sidelong at Maria. "I see you've done such a good job avoiding both those contingencies."

Eddy bristled. "Look, if you wanna make something of it—"

"No, no!" Carl held up his hand in surrender. "I have only the highest respect for an alarm that can mobilize a unit as quickly as it did you today." He caught Maria's eye with a hint of laughter in his own. Then suddenly the spark faded. He looked toward the lower bunk where, presumably, Camille slept, and his brows knotted together over his eyes. "How stupid of me! It never should have happened. Never *would* have happened if I'd been thinking straight . . ."

"Shut up, Carl!" Eddy growled, pricking the needle through a ragged flap of skin and drawing it through. He did not want to think about it, much less have Carl wax morbid on the subject. "Help me with this knot, will you?"

Carl leaned his chin over Eddy's arm. "I would, if you'd move your hand out of the way."

"If I move my hand, I'll lose the end. You've gotta— No—*Ouch, Carl!* Not that way; I won't have any skin left."

"Let me do it."

It was Camille. She had come up behind them unobserved. "It will be simpler for me to do it because my hands already know how to work together," she said, taking the needle and forceps from Eddy.

"I thought I told you to go to bed," Carl remembered.

"I can't sleep with all this racket."

It was true. They were plenty loud. "I'm sorry, Camille," Carl started.

"No, it's fine." She shrugged. "I overreacted. I guess I should have just taken the aspirin. It's just, I get sick if I take them too often." Camille's fingers kept up a steady pace as she talked, putting out neat knots of fishing line in Eddy's arm. Eddy's face held a slight grimace as his eyes followed her work.

"So I avoid aspirin when I can," Camille went on. "The pain's not bad right now. I just . . . I just want to go home!" Her chin trembled and she stared doggedly at Eddy's arm and kept stitching.

"Well," Carl decided after a strained moment. "Guess the fire could use another stick. Bit chilly in here." He got up and added a nicely seasoned log to the blaze and settled down on the floor to watch it burn. "Hey Jack, you got that thing working yet?"

Jack pulled his headset cord, and the crackling buzz of the radio filled the cabin.

"Not quite Guy Lombardo," said Carl, "but I'd settle for most anything at this point."

Jack went on adjusting knobs and dials. "You'll owe me dinner and a show when I introduce you to your new favorite."

"Yeah? And what'll that be?"

"Local police station," said Jack.

Carl chuckled. But the chuckle was short-lived. He looked around the cabin. Jack working. Maria cooking. Camille stitching. Eddy wincing. There had to be something he could do to take his mind off the pain. Something more helpful, that is, than banging his head against a wall or gouging his eye with a sharp stick. Or fork—the fork would be more convenient. There on the floor beside him were Eddy's breakfast dishes. Unwashed and sticky with jam and congealed egg yolk. Eddy would win no merit badges for that bit of work. Carl picked up the fork and absentmindedly drew stick figures in the yellow goo: a fellow with a big club whacking a kitty over the head. It was real art. Probably could have sold it for a buck or two, considering the rare medium. Egg yolk. Wait a minute! Egg yolk?

Carl snatched up the plate and jumped to his feet. "You're holding out on us, Eddy! Where'd you get the eggs?"

Eddy frowned. "What are you talking about?"

Carl shoved the dirtied plate toward his face. "You had eggs for breakfast. Now where'd you get them, and where'd you hide them? They don't grow on trees, you know!"

"Um, Carl, birds lay eggs," said biology professor Martin. "And so do frogs and fish and snakes and a few other things, if you really want to know. But," he pointed at the plate to emphasize each word: "I did *not eat eggs* for breakfast!"

"Come on, Eddy! Stop holding out on me! Can't you see what this means?"

"Sure. You're hungry."

"No!" Carl rolled his eyes. "It means that someone else has been—"

His explanation was cut off by a shriek. "Eddy! Oh Eddy, I saw its eyes!"

Forgetting the first-aid job that ought to be sterile, Eddy jumped from his chair. "Eyes? Whose eyes?"

Maria retreated to his arm. "A rat—over there in those boxes. It came out and glared at me with its horrid, wicked little face!"

"Why didn't you throw things at him?" Carl suggested. "Woulda kept him occupied until Eddy could shish kebab him on a needle!"

"Very funny!" Eddy sneered. Then, to Maria, "I guess it's gone now, Hon."

"Yeah, and too bad," Carl lamented. "You could've chopped him up and added him to the stew."

Both Eddy and Maria glared.

"What?" Carl shrugged. "Down-home cooking: just like Mama used to make." He smacked his lips and rubbed his stomach.

"Well then," said Maria, recovering herself. "I guess I'd better hurry up and get dinner served."

Camille touched Eddy's arm. "If you will hold still a few minutes more, I'll finish this up."

Eddy nodded and sat down again. Camille's handiwork was very neat and precise: one might even say dainty. Eddy remembered a few suturing jobs he had done that could have used her fine little fingers.

"Who taught you to stitch, Camille?"

Only then did her fingers falter. She looked up, met his eyes briefly. "My mother," she answered slowly. "There was always mending to be done with seven brothers about." She hurried to explain, lest Eddy think he was getting the same treatment as the torn overalls on wash day. "Mother taught me to sew: from there it was simple to pick up putting in a line of sutures."

But then, perhaps Eddy was not pleased. Perhaps his question had not been by way of commendation. Camille hesitated again before putting in the last few stitches.

Eddy nodded. "You do good work. You can stitch me up anytime—anytime I need it," he amended, as Maria placed a big pot of green bean soup on the table.

"Come and get it," she announced, setting places around in mismatched china and tin. Everyone gathered round the table, pulling up chairs and crates as necessary. A sorry lot they looked; every one among them was wearing a bandage of some kind, for Maria had burned her hand in the process of making supper. They sat down, and for a moment just stared at one another. Burns, blisters, concussed heads, broken bones, and all. They returned thanks and ate.

"I vote for an early retirement," said Eddy, slurping up the last of his meal.

"All right," Carl agreed, "but I hope you've been saving your pennies: don't think your pension counts for much out here."

"There are only two bunks," Eddy continued, wonderfully practiced at ignoring Carl's barbs. "But if the girls can share the top, we three can sleep crosswise on the—"

"Oh no!" Carl objected. "That bunk ain't wide enough for the three of us!"

Jack shook his head. "The only child speaks! When I was a boy, we shared six to a bunk, my brothers and I."

"You were slightly smaller then, Jack," said Eddy.

"And you didn't have a busted ribcage," Carl added. "I know how it will be: tall and skinny gets the middle and gets pummeled on either side by you gorillas. It's bad enough to have to share a bunk with a fellow who snores like an elephant with a stuffed-up nose, but when it comes to kickboxing, I'm out!"

"What do you mean?" Eddy grinned. "When it comes to kickboxing, you're the champ."

"Order, order!" Jack banged his tin cup on the table. "Carl and Eddy, you get the top bunk. The ladies will share the lower. I'll bed down near the door. No. No excuses. No bickering or further discussion. Just turn in and get some sleep. You all need it."

The group around the table broke up, each to prepare for another night. Carl moved to add more wood to the fire, cozying up to the blaze for a minute before turning in.

Camille settled down to the hearth near him. "Carl? What did Jack mean? When he said our chances depend on how much *we* want to get out?" She spoke in a whisper, now the only sound in the cabin except the crackling of the fire and the occasional groan from Eddy. "Doesn't he want to get out?"

"Oh, you know how it is. Life's rough. And sometimes . . ." Carl glanced over his shoulder at Jack bedded down on the floor and lowered his voice so Camille had to strain to hear his words. "He had a family, you know."

Camille shook her head. "No, I didn't."

Carl nodded. "He doesn't mention it. Not ever. I only heard because we were in sick bay together: he had fever and was going on. But yes, a family: wife, three little boys. Came home one day, found his house a black hole. All of them dead. Pearl Harbor. That sorta . . . killed part of him. Wish I'd known him before then: he musta been a swell guy. Look Camille, don't ever mention it to him."

Her eyes glowed with sympathy. "But sometimes it helps to talk about things."

"No, Camille. Let him work this one out."

She nodded. "All right."

They were silent a moment, then Carl drew a long breath.

"So. It's times like these that you start thinking: about things you've done and shouldn't have, words you said, things left undone that you maybe should have . . ." He looked earnestly at Camille. "Any regrets?"

She nodded. Carl waited for the great confession and prodded when it was not forthcoming.

She picked at a thread coming loose in her sleeve. "You won't like it, Carl."

"Try me."

"I wish I had accepted the captain's offer," she said.

"His offer?"

She shrugged. "Marriage."

Carl felt like Samson had tried to put a fist through his solar plexus. Maybe the strong man had succeeded. So that was it: Carl still played second fiddle to Captain Andrew Montgomery, Missing In Action.

A great fellow, the captain. He and Carl had shared a barracks for six weeks before Montgomery was shipped out. Carl felt they would have been close friends—if Montgomery had shipped out three weeks earlier: before he had met Camille. As it was, the mention of the captain's name stung Carl's teeth like vinegar. And all because Montgomery, a man of few words, made his words count. And Carl, who always said too much, somehow spoke too little.

"What about you, Carl?" Camille leaned closer. "Regrets?"

"Plenty," he said sourly. "I think I'll go to bed."

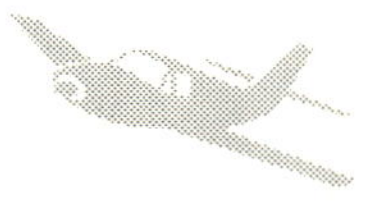

CHAPTER THIRTEEN

ROCKS

There were rocks in the mattress. And they caught him in the ribs: right where it hurt. Carl tried rolling over, wiggling one way, then the other. Nothing helped. Eddy yanked on the blanket and muttered in his sleep.

Try not to disturb Eddy. Poor fellow needs his sleep. Try to keep still. Lie still and sleep. Ignore the pain . . . and sleep!

Carl checked the time: 0445. He'd been fighting it for nearly two hours—ever since he'd been awakened by the cold and gotten up to retrieve Westman's jacket. Maybe it was the jacket that was so uncomfortable, not the mattress. He sat up and shucked it off, pitching it over the edge of the bunk. It landed with a *ka-whack!* on the floor. There followed the distinctive sound of two heads bonking the bottom of the upper bunk, and a piercing assault on the eardrums that would have raised the hair on the back of a dead man's neck. Eddy woke from his dead sleep, punishing his forehead against the ceiling, and added to the cacophony by demanding the reason for the screaming.

"It's down there! It's down there! I heard it!" Maria cried.

"What's down there? What is it? What's going on?"

Carl added his voice to the din: "It's nothing; just a flight jacket. I threw it over 'cause—*will you be quiet!*"

An electric torch flicked on from Jack's corner and the single word "Quiet!" rang out. Suddenly the shrill confusion was silent. Jack's torch beam cut the darkness until it lit upon the jacket.

"There it is! There it is! Oh, do something, please!"

"It's a leather jacket. It *won't eat you!*" said Carl. His former admiration for Maria's scream had melted away like butter on a hot day, leaving only a greasy tribute to something once helpful.

"But I heard it growling," Maria insisted. "There must be something in it."

"I was the last thing in it: if there was any growling going on, it woulda been me!"

"Okay, kiddies, everyone stay calm. It's Jack SuLong to the rescue." Jack rolled onto his stomach and pulled himself along the floor to the object in question, pausing when he got within distance to poke it with his crutch. "It appears to be quite dead," he assured Maria.

"But I heard it growl—"

Carl cut in with a voice which grew more bear-like with every word. "I threw it down because it was gouging me in the back: it may have landed hard, but it wasn't growling."

"Gouging you in the back?" Eddy questioned.

"Sure, sleeping in that thing is like sleeping on a pile of tin cans!"

"And how would you know about sleeping on tin cans?"

"After this," said Carl, "I know."

Jack pulled himself closer to the brown lump on the floor and gave it a few good swats. "No tin cans," he said.

"Well, maybe not cans, but rocks . . . or pebbles at least . . ." Carl sighed. "Look, I'm sorry: I woke everyone from their nice, restful slumber, and I'm sorry. Go ahead: pitch me out to feed the bears."

"Get over it, Carl," said Jack. "Ladies and gentlemen, this crisis is officially ended." The light clicked off. Several minutes passed in comparative silence as all tried to resume sleep. The fire crackled and popped with a sudden flicker of flame. Outside an owl called. The wooden bunk bed squeaked beneath Carl and Eddy as they shifted. Trees scraped against the cabin walls. A small animal scrambled past the door outside, returning to its nest after a night of feeding. Sleep would not come.

"All right, Carl," said Eddy. "Now you've got me wondering: just what *is* in that jacket?"

Jack's light was on in a flash. Eddy descended from the upper bunk and grabbed up the expensive scrap of cowhide that had caused so much unwarranted excitement.

"I don't feel any cans, rocks, *or* aircraft carriers in here, Carl. Pockets are empty—"

"Wasn't in the pockets," said Carl from his bunk.

"Nothing in the liner, either. Oh wait . . ."

Jack joined Eddy in the search for anything abnormal.

"Here's something about the size of a pea," said Eddy. "And rock hard."

"Here's another in the sleeve," Jack offered.

"I *told* you fellas it was full of rocks!"

"It's not *full* of rocks, Carl," Eddy corrected. "Just has a few too many for comfort."

"Hold it up," Jack suggested. "I always thought that shrimpy kid looked a bit built up in the shoulders. Aha. And feel: there's something in there." He drew out his knife.

"No, Jack, you can't," Eddy objected. "We should at least try to take the kid's belongings back to his folks."

"Oh sure: if we get back, the jacket gets back. And I happen to know someone who can stitch a neat seam, eh Camille?"

"If you can cut it straight, I'll stitch it straight," she answered, sitting up to watch.

"No guarantees there. Here, Eddy, hold the light." Jack's knife slid through the thread in the shoulder-seam lining. "There we go! Looks like a little white packet—an envelope, actually—buttoned up here in the shoulder to give a bulky, square silhouette. And—" Jack sliced the cloth envelope open and spilled the contents into his hand: a few tiny stones, glowing, sparkling, dancing with little rainbows on Jack's palm.

Maria gasped, and craned to get a better look.

"Well!" said Eddy, in awestruck appreciation of the gemstones.

Jack raised his eyebrows. "That's rather pretty."

"Ha!" Carl crowed. "I told you it was full of rocks!"

"But why would someone be carrying those around in their jacket liner?" asked Camille.

Maria's eyes still glowed with the sparkle of diamonds. "Wait a minute! Eddy: *the* Mr. Smith!"

"Back to that again, are we, Maria?"

"But it makes sense, doesn't it?"

"Sure," said Carl. "Big Smith plays his grandson for a chump, has him carry a few small items for him, arranges everything so the poor kid thinks he's all aboveboard and honest: probably gave him the jacket as a gift. And Walt, innocent as a lamb, doesn't know a thing if he gets caught. Why not?"

"You think Westman was played," said Eddy, leveling his gaze at each in turn. "What about us? Maybe this accident wasn't quite as accidental as it seemed."

"You've been making enemies with the wrong people, if that's the case," Carl quipped. "But let's pretend for a moment: suppose it *was* sabotage. Now . . . why us? And why Westman? If Westman was carrying those stones for Smith in all innocence, why would Smith crash the plane? Sorry, but it doesn't hold water."

"Who's to say Westman *was* innocent? He may have been pulling a fast one on his old man," Eddy suggested. "And who's to say it was Smith doing the sabotage?"

Carl grinned. "Enter, the unknown factor. What if 'X' and Smith were working together, but 'X' thinks Smith is giving him the double-cross—"

"Oh give it a rest!" Jack pleaded. "You boys could what-if the feathers right off a chicken!"

"Too bad for the chicken! At any rate," Carl yawned, "that little packet should solve all our problems."

"How's that?" Eddy was habitually the first to fall for one of his gags.

"Simple: ring up the Yellow Cab company, and advise that we'll pay *really* well for a ride back into town. *Voila!*"

Jack did not even crack a grin. "Great. That's why we keep you around, Carl. Here, Eddy, give me a hand up. It's nearly 0600, so I do believe I'll visit the little house down the trail and be back in time for breakfast. Save me some jam, will you, Carl?"

"Sure!" Carl agreed, still chuckling over his joke.

ꕥ ꕥ ꕥ

George Tumball slammed the door of his pickup truck and smiled at the shouts of young, playful voices in the backyard. Leaving his lunch pail by the front steps, he walked to the fenced-in patch of dried grass and chicken scratchings. Immediately, he was surrounded by a throng of six gun-toting cowboys and half-naked Indians wearing feathers and currant-juice warpaint, all hollering and whooping.

"All right, all right! What's going on here?" he asked, covering his ears at the din.

"We're playing cowboys and Indians," said one young man wearing freckles and a red bandanna. "But the Indians stole our last woman from camp and want to make her a squaw!" He pointed at a tow-headed girl sitting on an upturned bucket beneath the big oak, contentedly enjoying a fruit juice popsicle.

Uncle George's eyes sparkled as his hand sneaked into his pocket and withdrew a handful of peppermint candies. He scattered them on the ground, laughing as the stalwart ranchers and the warring tribe imitated the chickens, snatching them up and running to keep them from their fellows.

"There's one for each of you!" he called above the brouhaha. Turning, he walked toward the girl and nodded. "Evening, ma'am," he drawled.

She smiled until her cheeks dimpled, and plumped her yellow-flowered skirt with one hand. A dribble of melted popsicle slid down her chin.

"Do you happen to know where your brother Nick is?"

A fat finger pointed upward.

"Climbing trees, is he?" Tumball looked up to scan the golden leaf canopy.

The child giggled and shook her head, sending hair into her sticky face. Again she pointed up.

George frowned. "Suzie, have Frank and Nick gone flying?"

This time a nod. Without another word, Uncle George turned on his heel and raced for the house.

ꙮ ꙮ ꙮ

A little extra padding for the hip pocket, thought Vince Thomas as he stuffed a small wad of greenbacks into his wallet. A timely contribution too, what with the rent coming due that week. He stuffed the wallet into the pocket of his faded Levi's and bent to pick up his bag of mechanic's tools as the blue-and-white airplane rolled down the tarmac.

"They sure were in a fired-up hurry to be outta here," he muttered. "Wonder what—" he turned at the sound of an approaching car. A bright yellow star was painted on the side, and the words *Wayne County Sheriff.* Aw, nuts! What would it be this time? He'd paid his parking ticket, licensed the dog, and silenced the kids. What now? If anyone cared to know his opinion, he would say that Sheriff Kilroy was a killjoy.

"Mornin', Sheriff," Vince called, with a halfhearted attempt at good humor.

"Thomas," Kilroy nodded curtly as he stepped from his vehicle. "Got a call last night; decided to come talk to you about it first thing."

Vince winced. He, too, had gotten a call. Young Tommy Thomas and a friend had been out making trouble for a neighbor: something about tying a beef bone to the dog's tail and watching him chase after it until he spun himself right off his feet. It didn't really hurt anyone: the neighbor was cross, to be sure, but the dog recovered as soon as he was rewarded with the bone.

"Now look, Sheriff," Vince started to explain. "About last night—"

"Oh?" Kilroy's eyebrows lifted. "What about last night?"

"Well now, I don't know," said Vince, backtracking quickly. "What about that call you got?"

The airplane reached the top of the runway and sat there.

"I was told to be on the lookout for a couple of fellows; part of a smuggling ring, it's suspected."

"Oh really?" The wrinkles in Thomas's brow relaxed partly. "That's interesting. What'd they look like?"

"The descriptions were sort of sketchy," said the sheriff, pausing to scratch his nose. "The one was sort of medium height, medium build, with medium brown hair."

Thomas grinned. "Sheriff, if I didn't know better, I'd think you was talkin' about yourself!"

Kilroy was not amused. "And the other," he continued, "was a somewhat larger man, sort of jowley. That's about all the physical description I've got. The one distinguishing characteristic was they both spoke with an accent."

"Accent, huh? What sort?"

"Oh, I don't know. A foreign sort, I suppose."

"Ah yes, now that's very informative, Sheriff. Two men; one large, one medium, both with accent, both trying to escape a smuggling rap. I hate to break it to you, Sheriff, but . . ." He jerked a thumb over his shoulder as the aircraft rolled forward, picking up speed. "I think those are your men."

ꝏ ꝏ ꝏ

"I'm very sorry," Orville informed Rigby, as he reentered the room. "Mr. Smith is ill and will not be taking visitors."

The butler did a double take at the sight of Harry Jensen occupying a chair with his feet propped up on a low table.

"Hi, Orville. Remember me? Oh yeah, I let myself in. Normal people who don't have butlers do it all the time: wonderful inventions, these doorknobs! Now why don't you trot on back to Smith's hideout where he's nursing his ego and a bottle of whiskey, and see if he isn't too sick to see his old friend Harry. That's right, there's a good boy."

Orville left the room and was back in two minutes, a frown agitating his normally placid face. "Mr. Smith is recovered enough to have a short visit."

"Right. Thanks a bunch, Orville!" Harry pressed past the butler with Rigby tight on his heels.

Milford was slumped in his oversized chair, facing the empty fireplace. He made no move at the sound of his visitors entering. The unraveled strings on the cuffs of his green robe mirrored his unraveling plans as he reached to pour himself another drink, sans the soda.

"You ratted on me, Harry," he griped.

"Nope," Harry replied calmly from behind. "I haven't said a word. Yet."

"I don't care what you say! Or you, either!" Smith growled, turning on Inspector Rigby, who had been about to speak. "I've been in worse scrapes before, but I've gone on for years against the odds without any convictions because anyone who knew anything was too scared to rat; and the ones that weren't, I took care of them! You understand, Harry, I took care of them."

Harry nodded. "I understand, Smith. Perfectly."

Milford gulped his drink and poured again, settling deeper into his drunken state as he did the same into his chair.

"As a matter of fact, Mr. Smith, it was your mechanic, Benny Ferguson, who squealed on you." Rigby strolled to another chair and plopped down.

"Fool!" Milford hissed, a sudden spark lighting his red eyes.

"Yessir, nice little story he told: all about a bathtub full of holes!"

A gurgling chuckle rose from Milford's throat, and his whole belly shook as he laughed. "Ah yes, Inspector, you like that one?"

"Yes, actually. Very interesting trick: only too bad it backfired! Oh, you didn't know?" Rigby asked, reading Milford's startled reaction. "Yes, it backfired. The planes were switched, Milford. Your boy was on that plane."

Milford sat in shocked silence, then glanced furtively at Harry.

Harry, looked from one to the other of them. "All right, what does it mean? What about the planes? Answer me!"

Milford shook his head. "Walter went down on that plane," he whispered to himself. "It's the beginning of the end for me." He heaved himself to his feet and gathered up his bottle and tumbler as if for one more drink. Then with a sudden speed and precision which no one would have accused him of possessing, Milford flung the heavy tumbler at Harry's face. He charged Rigby with the bottle.

The tumbler was prevented from doing serious damage to Harry's face by colliding with his nose. Whiskey stung his eyes, but he drew his service pistol and fired at a target that was too big to miss.

Rigby had no time even to spring from his chair. He ducked his head to the side, avoiding the blow of the bottle. It broke on the back of the chair at almost the same instant the report of Harry's gun was heard. Milford's body tumbled forward into Rigby's lap. The legs of the overstrained chair gave out and the chair crunched backward to the floor. There was a quick moment of profound silence. Then Rigby, pale and shaking, struggled out from under the crushing weight. The tinkling of broken glass accompanied his movements as he shook the shards from his coat. "You're pretty handy with that pistol," he remarked, relieved that his broken mug would *not* be appearing in a police file marked *Whiskey Murders.*

Harry was wiping furiously at the alcohol in his eyes with the back of his fist. Blood drained from his nose and down his chin; his gun still trained in the general direction of his last shot. Rigby became conscious of his awkward position and extricated himself quickly from the line of fire.

"Hey! You know you could have killed me, shooting blind like that!"

"'Could have' and 'did' are two entirely different things," Harry pointed out. He plucked the handkerchief from Rigby's pocket. "Now what about that airplane?"

ꙮ ꙮ ꙮ

George stepped across the threshold. "They've gone up." It was less question and more statement.

From his chair in the living room, his brother Adam nodded dispiritedly. "Yes." He frowned at the two white plaster casts poking from beneath the blanket on his lap. "I told him not to go: told him to wait. He wouldn't listen. And I . . . useless . . . helpless to stop him!"

"When?"

"Nick left nearly three hours ago," said Adam's wife.

George frowned. There was not fuel enough for three hours' flight. Either they were in trouble or . . . George shook his head. No. They were in trouble: it was Frank's way of doing things.

Just then, his wife Loretta appeared from the kitchen and offered a round of lemonade. "What can we do?" she asked, setting aside the empty drink tray. Her voice was calm, but she pressed her lips together in a straight line, suppressing inner panic.

George took a long drink. "First we have to stay calm."

"I don't understand what's gotten into him!" Adam declared, slapping the arm of his chair. "He's never been like this before."

George sighed. Adam had it easy: Nick was usually mild-mannered and tractable. Frank, on the other hand, had been a trial ever since his father was killed in the war and George had married his widowed mother. It was not unusual for Frank to do something stupid. But now he was endangering his cousin with him. George took one last drink and set it aside. "All right, I'm gonna get down to the airport and see if anyone knows anything. Then I'll find a plane, go up, take a look around."

"Be careful, George," Loretta pleaded.

George nodded. "I'll bring those boys home," he promised.

CHAPTER FOURTEEN

DROP-IN COMPANY

It was time for breakfast. Maria insisted on fixing pancakes. This was good. The waiting was not. To keep Carl out of her way, she gave him the task of sifting through the flour and removing all the tiny dead bugs while she readied the kitchen for duty.

"A little extra protein never hurt anyone," Carl complained.

"If you want to eat raw flour, go ahead," Maria replied with a slight toss of her head. "But I'm not having bugs in my pancakes."

Fine. If that's how it had to be, that's how it would be. Carl knew better than to argue with the cook. He resigned himself to sorting through six cups of flour for bugs that would hardly add a crunch. He paused a moment, his hand dusted white; his eyes lit upon an old dead beetle that lay drying on the counter. It was a good two inches long. Carl snagged it and dropped it into the bowl.

"I think I got them all."

"I'll be there in a minute," said Maria.

Carl smiled to himself. Then—whoops! The dead beetle came to life, digging for all it was worth. Carl reached for it but not before it was burrowed beneath the flour. Maria arrived at his elbow and picked up the bowl.

"Uh, wait there's uh . . ."

She paused. "Yes?"

Carl changed his mind. "Oh, nothing. Just . . . nothing."

Maria frowned, then shrugged, and whisked the bowl away.

Carl would know his breakfast when he saw it: there would be a big black beetle in it, fried alive. Not that he cared. He leaned his forehead on the table and closed his eyes.

From the top bunk came the sound of Eddy's purring snore; a soft sigh from Camille on the lower bunk with her ankle elevated. Maria was happy in her work, as evidenced by her low humming; as yet, blithely unaware of Carl's sabotage. Jack had not yet returned to the cabin.

Carl gritted his teeth. He couldn't think to do anything else. Nothing but hurt. And bug the pancakes. The pain was really getting to him. Had he grown so soft in two years? That was embarrassing.

The cabin door started open and Carl lifted his head, trying to compose a smart remark for Jack. Except it wasn't Jack. Surprised, Carl stood. Help had come!

Or had it?

The visitor did not look friendly. Neither did his Springfield.

A big, scruffy fellow, beard and hair unkempt and grown long; his hard grey eyes looked long at Carl before sweeping the room.

"Hello, friend," said Carl, taking a forward step which put him in the direct line of fire.

Silent, the eyes studied him again.

"We're all friendly here, so if you would point that—"

From the top bunk came the eruption that was Eddy. "Pack your bags, girls! We're going home!" He catapulted from the bunk and landed with his knees bent. Upon straightening, the newcomer's Springfield introduced itself face to face.

"Hey—" Eddy glanced at Carl with a nod toward their visitor. "What's wrong with him?"

"Worms for breakfast," Carl muttered. "It'll do it to anyone."

A slow line of humor crept up the gunman's face, twitching his mouth until he let out a chuckle. He stood his rifle in the corner by the door and his chuckle grew into a full-blown laugh. Carl and Eddy joined in, relieved that the Springfield had not delivered the punchline.

"Say," Eddy began, "I thought for a moment—"

"But only for a moment," Carl cut in. "That's typical of you, Eddy."

"Drop-in company," the man mused, divesting himself of the pack he carried. He laid it aside and proceeded to unbutton, first, a soiled sheepskin coat, and then a heavy flannel jacket. These he removed as one garment, leaving the sleeves pulled inside-out, appearing before them a much smaller man than Carl had originally thought. Tugging off a moth-eaten cap, he grinned wolfishly, as one a little out of practice with the exercise.

"Forgive me, I'm a little slow. You caught me off guard."

"You seemed pretty well on it to me," Eddy observed.

The man laughed outright, an act which brought to light the heretofore disguised handsomeness of his rugged face. "Let me try again then," he said with an open-handed gesture. "Welcome! And make yourselves at home. It looks like you've had a rough time of it, but I hope your stay here will be as comfortable as possible."

"What we'd really like," said Carl, "is to get *out* of here as soon as possible."

The man nodded. "That can be arranged."

"Well, that's okay then," Eddy acknowledged with a nod. "Say, I'm Eddy Martin. And that's Carl Linder . . . My wife, Maria . . . Camille Jensen . . ."

The man shrugged. "You can call me most anything, as long as it's not late for supper. I go by Jack."

"Well, that's funny," said Eddy, "because we have a—"

"—Our dog," Carl cut in quickly. "Back home. He goes by Jack, too." He grinned. "Even comes to it occasionally."

Eddy laughed and glanced sidelong at Carl.

Maria called from the kitchen. "If you're not too busy, boys, you could come have some breakfast."

"Sounds good to me," the new Jack declared. He straddled a bench and cocked an eye at the pretty waitress who set a plate of pancakes in front of him. "Not bad," he nodded. "Not bad at all. I'm gone for a couple of days to resupply, and I come home to good food and a—"

Eddy cleared his throat loudly. "How soon can we be out of here?" he asked.

Jack's ogling continued as Maria brought more food to the table. He cut a bite and crammed it into his mouth, chewing slowly.

"The radio!" Eddy snapped his fingers. "As soon as Jack has it going—"

"It's no good," Jack answered with his cheek distended. "Battery's dead."

Again, Eddy's sideways glance at Carl.

"You can all tuck up here," said Carl, talking fast as the plans came to him. "I'll hit the mountain tomorrow. With enough food and supplies, I should be able to make good on a trek for help."

Jack eyed Carl a second. A corner of his mouth twitched and his eyebrow shot up. "Yes," he nodded, studying Carl again. "Yes. It's a good plan. But double your chances: if both of you go—"

Eddy made an unmistakable noise in his throat, and Jack let the suggestion drop.

"All right then," said Carl with a confident nod. "I guess that settles it." He stared a long moment at Camille. She held one corner of her lip in her teeth as if it were a trap. "I'll start tomorrow," he added.

Maria joined them at the table. "Tell us about yourself, Mr. Jack. How did you come to be here?"

Jack smiled and stuck out his tongue to lick the sticky from his fork. "It's a long story," he began. "It starts with my great-great-grandpa. You see, we've been here for generations. Simple folk, us. Living offa just what we can reach. Harvesting some timber—"

Carl laughed and jerked his head at Eddy. "Simple folk—I'll bet he don't know the war's over!"

Raising his eyebrows, Jack looked from one to the other between Eddy and Carl, that half-grin tugging at his rugged features. "War?"

ᘓ ᘐ ᘓ

A deep furrow ran the length of George's brow. He sat for a minute, tapping his thumb rapidly on the steering wheel to relieve his nervous energy. No one had been of any help at the airfield. Sure, they'd seen Frank and Nick; seen them go up in the red Cessna 140; seen them fly merrily on their way. Now where in the world did you start a search for a two-person airplane? The task loomed large and hopeless. George banged his fist on the rim of the wheel.

"Frank! Why'd you have to be so stubborn? It's bad enough when you risk your own neck, but now you've got your cousin gummed up in it, too! What am I going to tell your mum? Your aunt and uncle?"

He shook his head. He would just have to start where he could. Putting the truck in gear, George pulled from the airport parking lot and onto the highway. He would stop by the police department to file an alert, then head on up the mountain to see if anyone had noticed a small red airplane.

༄ ༄ ༄

"More of Frank's shenanigans, eh?"

George nodded and sighed. "Yes, only it's worse this time: he's got Nick with him."

The clerk frowned and shook her head. "That boy!"

"Yes, that boy. Now Gina, please, would you just keep an eye out for me? Tell me if you hear something? Because, frankly, I don't know where to begin."

She looked at her brother over the rims of her glasses, unaffected by his desperation.

George nearly exploded. "Oh for pity's sake, Gina! Can't you do something? This is my son we're talking about!"

"Your *step*son," Gina corrected languidly, and she picked up the telephone that was ringing on her desk. "Yes, what is it?"

George gripped the countertop with both hands, thinking he just might rip it off and tear it to pieces unless he got some action.

Gina continued in her sleepy tone. "Huh? Red airplane, you say? Dumped in the pond, eh? Oh, and two boys pulled out. We'll look into it . . . Carter's pond," she said to George, replacing the receiver.

"Carter's pond!" George shouted. "Gina, you old sourpuss, you're wonderful!" He heaved himself up on the counter, leaned over to kiss her on the cheek, and was on his way again before she could say a word.

Gina sat staring after him for five seconds, the barest hint of a smile twitched at the corner of her frowning mouth. Then shaking her head, she reset her face in its customary scowl, preparing for her next victim.

"Complaint? Name? Your name?"

CHAPTER FIFTEEN

CATCH OF THE DAY

The Carter brothers' half-blind bluetick bayed joyfully, circling, and nearly tripping George as he dashed for the porch. Barely knocking, George burst through the door, demanding to know where his boys were. Dick Carter, an elderly man with rather disheveled white hair, wearing a rather tattered flannel shirt, kindly disregarded his unconventional entrance, and jerked a thumb toward the kitchen where two forms sat in front of steaming bowls of soup, shrouded in woolen blankets.

Frank, who since turning fifteen was too old to shed a tear, burst into sobs. "I'm sorry, Dad! I'm sorry!" he bawled, dropping into George's arms.

Dad. First time he'd been called Dad by his eldest boy. George wrapped his arms around him. "It's okay," he soothed. "I'm just glad you're both all right."

"I'm sorry about the plane!" Frank howled.

George winced. Doubtless it was sunk. He felt himself sink a little. This would be the end of the flying era.

"We'll discuss that later," he said. And then added, "I'm just glad you're not hurt," partly as a reminder for his own benefit. He looked up at Mr. Carter. "I hope they didn't cause any damage, sir, but if they did, why I'll pay for—"

"Not at all," said Mr. Carter. "Airplane'll make fine fish habitat. Been meanin' to throw some junk in the pond for the fish. Looks like they took care of that for me."

The elder Carter brother, Gary, a man with very disheveled white hair and wearing a very tattered flannel shirt, piped up from the end of the table. "Best fishin' we've had in years! Caught two big 'uns!"

George smiled wanly, now anxious to get home. "I'm very grateful to you for pulling them both out—"

"Yup! Good thing we was right there in the boat, or them boys would've gone right down with the plane!" Gary Carter crowed. He leaned his chair back, hooked his thumbs in imaginary suspenders, and was about to wax eloquent in story when George excused himself.

"Come on boys, we need to get you on home and let your folks know you're okay." It took some effort to disentangle themselves from the clutches of the kindly Carter brothers and get out to the pickup. For some minutes there was a strained silence, and then:

"I saw an old airstrip, and a crashed plane, and there were people signaling!" Nick declared.

Frank groaned.

George glanced at his nephew for slightly longer than he should have while driving on the twisting, washboarded road. "Come again?"

"Frank thought it was lightning, but I saw people, and they were signaling, and needed help, and I'm pretty sure if they don't get help they'll all die."

"Nick, I told you it wasn't—"

"Where?" George wanted to know.

"I don't know," Nick admitted. "There were a lot of trees."

"Frank?"

Frank shrugged. "I don't know. I wasn't paying attention."

"There were a few other things you weren't paying attention to," Nick chided. Given that they were safe on earth once more, he felt secure to do so. "It was near the old cabin, remember?"

"What cabin?"

"Don't tell me you didn't see the cabin!"

"Nick!" Frank hissed. "I was busy flying, not sight-seeing!"

"Well, if you'd looked around a little more you would have seen that old airstrip and we wouldn't be soaking wet from the pond!"

"Did you really want me to try to land where someone else had just crashed?"

"Well . . . no. But I didn't want you to land in the pond, either."

"Which is why you were screaming all the way down."

"I wasn't screaming!" Nick protested. "I was just a little excited, that's all."

"You were screaming," Frank sneered. "Which, by the way, makes it really hard to concentrate."

"I was *not* screaming!" Nick shrieked. And showing a bit of temper, he smacked his cousin on the side of the head. Frank returned the blow and the fight escalated in a matter of seconds before George called for order.

"Boys, boys! Cut it out, or you can walk home!" His eyes followed the road but his mind took a new trail of thought. "A cabin . . . and an old strip . . . There's an old Forest Service outfit back there; I wonder if . . . Well," he decided at last, "it might bear some looking into."

ꕥ ꕥ ꕥ

"Carl!" Camille's voice was fierce in its softness.

"What?" He barely moved his lips to form the syllable.

"You can't go!"

"Says who?" he challenged.

She pressed her lips tight together. "We need you."

His eyes flitted around the room as much as to say, "*You'll be fine.*"

"But I . . . you're not . . ." She scraped back her chair and went for a plate of hot pancakes. Returning, she tossed two of them onto Carl's plate. He passed one of them on to Other Jack; it had little black legs sticking out of it.

Other Jack looked up at Camille and winked. "Oh thanks, sweetie."

Carl's fist nearly had a convulsion.

Other Jack spread his pancake with jam before cutting it and stuffing it into his mouth. Carl watched it go down, bite by bite.

"So there I was," Other Jack continued, "with the she-bear between me an' the nearest tree, an' me between her an' the cubs . . ." His pancake crunched between his teeth, and he paused to examine it with his tongue. With a slight shrug, he went on chewing and swallowed. He continued his story; Eddy and Maria sat listening, Eddy's hand protectively clasped over Maria's on the table in front of them.

Carl heard it first: a gentle, lilting melody, one of Jack's favorite tunes. The words were a mystery in some island tongue. Jack had said it was something about a fish and a princess.

"Ah!" Eddy slid his chair back and turned toward the door. "Here's Jack," he said.

"Jack? Your dog?" Other Jack raised his eyebrows. "He sings very nicely," he said.

The singing came closer, Jack's smooth voice carrying the tune in a rich tenor. At last he flung wide the cabin door and delivered his last line in broad performance. He made an awkward bow amid applause and stomping.

"Any jam left?" Jack asked. "I see there's company."

"Yes, and it's us," said Carl, rising for the occasion. "Jack, I'd like to present Jack: he lives here. In fact, his father lived here, and his grandfather before him, way back to great-great-grandpappy Columbus. We've just been very hospitable, showing him a good time, and sharing his food with him. Now you see what those eggs meant, Eddy?"

Jack looked at their host and reached out his hand. "Well, well, this *is* a surprise. Let me think, it's Atgood, isn't it? Joseph Atgood. Go by Joe? No, sorry, you said Jack. But that's a bit awkward now that there's two of us, yes?"

Other Jack's outstretched fingers curled into his palm. "You have a good memory for faces," he acknowledged slowly.

"Have I?" asked Jack. "It's better for headlines. How's this one: 'Embezzler caught in war office' Or this one: 'Atgood maims cop; flees.'"

Eddy snapped to his feet, he and Carl flanking Atgood.

"Atgood!" Carl stormed. "So that's why he looked so familiar!"

"Why you dirty crook!" Eddy snarled. "I mighta known: any woodsman worth his salt knows the difference between a lodgepole and a larch! Pretty lot of stories you tell, and all lies!"

Maria added her contribution: "You shouldn't say a radio battery is dead when it isn't, Mr. Atgood. It makes a person question your truthfulness."

Jack smiled. "Well, Mr. Atgood, you've long enjoyed living here at government expense, haven't you? Then I have good news for you, because prison will look pretty swanky after this. I understand they have excellent room service."

"Very clever, all of you," said Atgood. "Just one thing." He tore the shirt free of his waistband. His hand leveled a 9 millimeter at Eddy's chest. "Here you, dollface!" he shouted at Maria. "Get over here!"

Eddy lurched forward.

"Not so fast!" Atgood glowered. "Not unless you want to top off breakfast with lead!"

He grabbed Maria by the neck, forcing the gun muzzle against her temple. "There now: that seems nice and cozy, don't it?"

"Eddy!"

"Yes. Eddy!" Atgood mocked in falsetto. "I tried to play nice with you: tried to defend your sweet, innocent eyes from things you shouldn't see. I wanted to send you all away to live 'happily ever after.' How'd that work for me?" He nodded at Jack. "Then *you* have to show up and spoil it for everyone. Nice going, Jack! Very nice. I'm sure your friends appreciate you now."

"Stop while you're ahead, Atgood," Jack warned. "You haven't killed anyone yet. Not even that cop. Don't get stuck with a murder charge now."

Atgood showed his teeth. "Don't bargain with me! I've already been down that road. And I don't plan to get stuck with any mur—"

A noise from the corner. Atgood turned his head. Camille had scuffed her brace as she approached him from behind, a heavy length of firewood clutched in her hand. With a snarl, he brought his gun arm across her face; a vicious blow that dropped her cold.

With a shout, Carl hurled himself for Atgood's throat. His fingers caught and crushed. Atgood stumbled backward. The gun lifted.

Jack struck Carl from the side with the power of a tsunami. Carl fell just before two shots exploded. Jack dropped to the floor.

Eddy made a dive for Atgood's legs and took a hard-soled boot to the chin. Atgood was out the door, Carl in pursuit. He snatched up Jack's pistol and fired at the retreating figure: once for he and Eddy, once for Maria, twice for Camille. And the remaining three for Jack.

ꕥ ꕥ ꕥ

Smoke curled from Harry Jensen's ears as he slid the auto into a parking space, sharing paint with the car beside. His office assistant, Felix Bateman, sat in the passenger seat screaming silently and clutching at the door. Harry was exiting before they jerked to a complete stop.

"Roll out 739 Alpha Tango."

"B-but who's going to f-fly it?" Bateman protested, hands shaking as they tried to work the door handle.

Harry did not stop to chat as he started prepping 424 Echo Mike. "You are."

"But . . . but I don't . . ."

"You are," Harry repeated. He continued work on Echo Mike, annoyed at the sight of a man approaching with purposeful tread. Salesman, probably: no time for that.

"Excuse me, mister."

"Get lost!" Harry answered politely.

The tall stranger was undaunted. He pulled a couple bills from his wallet. "I'm looking to rent a plane."

"Get outta here! Bates, get moving!"

"But it's important!" the stranger pressed.

Harry pointed first at the stranger, then at Bateman, supplying a word for each. "Get! Move!"

"My son and nephew were flying our two-place and they saw what looked like a crash, and people signaling for help—"

"Where?" Harry looked down and realized he had grabbed the man by his shirt collar. He modified his behavior for a gentler line of attack. "Where?"

The stranger pulled back, brushing the creases from his work shirt. He seemed hesitant now to tell at all.

Harry pointed at 739 Alpha Tango, a four-place Beechcraft Bonanza. "Tell me where, and she's yours!"

The man staggered at the offer. "Mine . . . to rent for the day?"

"No. Yours, yours! Can you tell me where?"

"No, I just had a sort of guess; I wanted to go up and look—"

"Can you fly a Bon?"

"Maybe, I guess; I don't know."

"Bateman, give him the keys!"

Suddenly off the hook, Bateman helped the stranger prep 739 Alpha Tango and then stood aside to watch as both craft left the ground. He turned back to the car in time to see an unhappy man surveying the damage to his paint. Bateman groaned and reached for his wallet.

CHAPTER SIXTEEN

SAME TREE

Carl paused for a moment in the doorway, afraid to know the truth. Gathering himself together, he stepped inside. Jack was on his back on the floor. Maria was tucking a blanket over his body, Eddy placing a pillow under his head.

Eddy looked up at Carl. "Did you get him?" His usually placid face whiplashed between anger and fear.

Carl shook his head in shame and knelt by Jack. "Hey, buddy. Why is it you always get to do the honors?"

Jack opened his eyes briefly and grunted in reply.

From the place where she'd fallen, Camille sat up, pressing a wax-like hand to the side of her head. Carl crossed to her and dropped to his knees. "Camille. Darling. Okay?"

She nodded.

"If we get out of here, remind me to ask you something important."

Surprise lit her face, and then the slightest hint of a smile. "Remind me to say 'yes.'"

For a bare second Carl clasped her hand. "It's a deal!"

"Carl!" Eddy's voice rang with alarm. He wiped his forehead and his hand came away wet. "I've got to get those slugs out of him! Fetch the med chest, Carl. Maria! Boiling water."

Jack's hand came up and gripped Eddy's arm. "Don't waste time on me," he insisted.

"No." Eddy shook his head. "No, Jack. Not a second. Camille, can you . . . ?"

With a quick affirmative, she slid across the floor as Carl brought the chest and placed it near the operating table. Eddy looked up, painful uncertainty creasing his brow.

Carl nodded. "Carry on, Doc."

Eddy tried to swallow. "Pray hard," he replied.

❧ ❧ ❧

"Buttons, buttons everywhere: now which one should I push?" George's fingers hovered over the dashboard while the radio crackled with Harry's voice.

"What's our heading? I asked for a heading! Hey! What kind of a maneuver was that? You're flying an airplane, not a kite!"

George resumed an upright attitude. "Radio, radio, wherefore art thou, radio? Aha!" He pushed the button on the yoke. "We'll try a northeast heading. If I'm not mistaken, there's a Forest Service strip in the back forty somewhere. That might be what Nick was talking about." George cast a glance at his flying companion. There was definitely something missing on that airplane. "Say, is that one of them newfangled fancy airplanes that pick up their wheels in flight, or do you have bad problems?"

"It's called retractable landing gear. There's a lever marked 'landing gear.' Use it."

George shifted the control and felt the whirring vibration of the landing gear lifting. "Well I'll be! Isn't that keen? Never flown something so fancy before! Not used to all these funny knobs and gadgets. When Pop and I were flying the back country, we just had a fuel gauge and a compass!"

"You can go back to your paper airplanes later," Harry growled. "Right now we've got work to do!"

"Sure thing, Boss!" George smiled. He could get used to this!

ജ ଓ ഇ

Nerves of steel, that's what Camille had. She had barely flinched as she assisted Eddy in the surgery. Intent through the whole process, her demeanor unmoved, she had responded promptly to the doctor's instructions with steady fingers.

Carl pressed his head against the doorjamb, trying to catch a breath of air. Was it just him, or had the world gone pale and out of focus? It wasn't that blood bothered him so much; just the fact that it was Jack's blood.

Eddy was still kneeling over his patient. "Not yet, Jack," he was saying. "Your chariot's not coming yet."

"I hear it," Jack protested. "Hear it . . ."

Carl turned back to the open doorway, his throat tightening. So this was it for Jack: he'd given up. If the fight was gone from him . . .

He ought to bid him goodbye; say something at least. *Thanks for getting us out of this scrape; for being a true friend. For teaching bravery and honor . . .* How could you say things like that in just a few minutes? How could you briefly acknowledge a life given, poured out, for another? *Greater love hath no man than this . . .*

"Hear it coming," Jack repeated, louder.

"Stick with me, Jack!" Eddy encouraged. "Jack!"

Camille gasped. "I hear it too!"

The cabin went silent. Surely it was the imagination. The wind in the trees? A hungry stomach growling? Surely not—

"Signal flares!" Eddy cried.

Carl leaped up, grabbed the bag of pistol and flares, raced for a clearing in the trees. He ran a cross-country mile in ten minutes. When he paused halfway to catch a breath there was blood in his mouth. By the time he reached an opening where he could shoot, he was coughing up more. He sat down, double images swaying before his eyes; mechanically loaded the pistol and fired. Loaded and fired. Loaded and fired. The sound of the engine seemed closer. He loaded the fourth round, fired, and fainted.

ꟷ

Streams of water ran up the Beechcraft's windshield. Visibility was lost in the sludge of grey haze. Down, down, below the clouds; nearly scraping their bellies on the endless trees. George wondered when Harry would lose his nerve. There was no sign of that yet. The radio squalled.

"Confounded soup! Seen anything?"

"Nothing. What do you say we go up and wait for this to blow over?"

Silence. Then finally: "You can head back if you want; I'll stick it out a while longer."

"Can't go much lower—"

"Then cut out!" Harry interrupted. "I'm going to find them!"

"I was going to say," George continued, "that we can't go much lower without some pretty fancy flying, but I'm game, if you are."

"Right then. We'll continue round this peak and—wait a minute!"

"Well!" George admired the red sparkles floating in the sky. "That looks like the Fourth of July!"

"Only it's no picnic. Looks like we've found them," said Harry. "Let's get down."

"They're coming in!" Eddy handed a blanket each to Camille and Maria. "Take these and head down." Taking a third himself, he spread it on the floor beside Jack and eased his friend onto the stretcher. Then he grabbed Camille's bag, dumped it, and stuffed it beyond capacity with medical supplies.

Sinking to the floor, he pressed Jack's hand between his own. "Come on, Jack. You can't give up on me now!"

There was not even a flutter of movement to accompany Jack's response. "You kids . . . fine now."

"No. No, Jack! I need you to make it for me." He pressed the hand tighter. "Don't die on me, Jack!"

The sound of engines droned loud. Wrenched by a sob, Eddy tore himself from Jack's side, pausing at the open door. "Hear that, Jack? Your chariot's coming to take us all home. Hang in there!"

A blue-and-white Bonanza hove into view, banked to set up for landing. From somewhere on the trail below, Maria screamed. Eddy's face twisted in horror as the airplane made for the same tree that had brought them down.

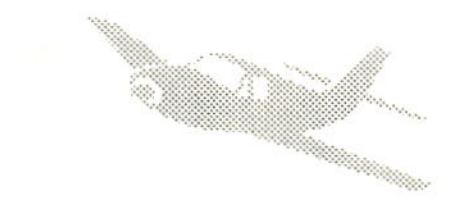

CHAPTER SEVENTEEN

SAFE AS A BABY'S CRADLE

With a cry, Camille darted forward and dropped by Carl's side. He was slumped over a rock, the flare pistol still tight in his grasp. Blood bubbled softly from his nose with each breath. Camille turned him onto his side so it would drain and tucked the blanket over him. Her hand sought his wrist and that delicate thread of life still pulsing in him.

Maria screamed.

❧ ❧ ❧

"Watch out!" George yelled. He saw Harry's plane jerk to a knife edge and pull out sharply, yielding the airstrip to him. George did a low pass, observing the overgrown field, the trees that made him want to pull in his elbows, the scattered pieces of an airplane, crumpled like paper.

"Well then," he said to himself, "this will be a ride."

His radio made some ugly traffic. "Listen you, if you try landing that boat without your landing gear, I won't *need* to murder you!"

George rectified his near mistake as he banked to make final, and once more felt the shudder of the gear as it swung into place. Wheels met the ground. The airplane bucked and pitched like an ornery horse colt. George braced in the seat, fighting for control of the yoke. Finally coming to a stop, he taxied to one side to clear the field for Harry.

A woman's voice called for help. George ran toward it.

"The cabin . . ." she gasped, panting hard. "Our friend is hurt."

George ran on and met a man who turned with a wave and a yell. "Help me with Jack!"

ꟷ ꟷ ꟷ

Camille looked up. "Uncle Harry? How . . . ?"

"What happened?"

"Carl's hurt."

Harry looked. Yes. Badly. He gathered Carl, still unconscious, into his arms and loaded him into his plane. Eddy and George returned with Jack on the blanket between them and secured him in the other. All boarded.

"You new?" Eddy asked the pilot.

"Uh, sort of," George replied.

"Ever fly a Bon before?"

"Nope."

"Well, set her down easy, would you?" Eddy closed his eyes. "I'm too tired to do that bit again."

ⵗ ⵗ ⵗ

Harry had two ambulances waiting when they arrived at the airport. One for Jack; Camille with Carl in the other. Eddy jumped from the cockpit to help load. Rounding the nose, he ran into the prop with his head. He backed up and tried again, feeling his way around this time.

The medics had Carl nearly ready for transport. He'd lost a lot of blood, but was semi-responsive, twitching at the sound of Eddy's voice. There was something Carl had to know: something that Eddy, if he never had another chance to speak with him again, needed him to know. He put a hand on Carl's shoulder as he lay on the gurney and leaned close. "You got him, Carl," he said. "You got him."

Then they whisked Carl away. Eddy watched the ambulance drive off. Five out of six. They'd made it out. Whether two of them would live to tell about it was another question. That was out of his hands now: he'd done what he could. Had he done right? If Jack were to die because of some error he'd made, how could he live with himself?

Eddy shook his head. He couldn't think about that now. His mind was numb. He needed to sit down. The world was whizzing out of control as he started to sink down on the tarmac. Harry arrested his attempt, grabbing his arm.

"Come on, Eddy," he said, hauling him back to his feet. "Let's get you to the doc."

"Okay," Eddy nodded. "I'll wait here."

"You do that," Harry responded with a knowing nod. He walked Eddy to his car and seated him beside a beautiful woman. Eddy leaned his head on her shoulder.

"When the bough breaks, the cradle will fall . . . See, Maria, safe as a baby's cradle."

ꕥ ꕥ ꕥ

"Characterized by confusion, momentary lapses in memory, impaired judgment, and sudden erratic behavior . . ."

It was an odd conversation to wake up to. Eddy opened one eye; the other was locked shut under layers of bandages. He stared at the two white lab coats that stood across the room with their backs to him. Two identical lab coats. The only difference he could see was in the shape of the heads that poked out the top: one was thick and close shaven, the other thin with plenty of hair. They were studying a picture of the inside of someone's skull. Most likely, Eddy realized, it was his own.

He closed his eye again and sank back into the comfort of the flattened hospital mattress, enjoying the feel of clean, scratchy, army-surplus pajamas. He wasn't going to take a diagnosis of "sudden and erratic" sitting down. No siree! They'd be fortunate if they got him out of bed in a month.

He sighed deeply and was on the verge of sleep when a thought popped into his head that woke him quicker than a direct IV of night-mission coffee: Jack! With a loudly uttered exclamation to that same effect, Eddy dislodged the hideous green bedspread and bolted for the door. The lab coats turned in unison—my, my, they had faces on front!—and dropped their jaws on the floor. Eddy felt a little bad for startling them so; but with a patient who is prone to sudden and erratic behavior, they should have been prepared. This should teach them a valuable lesson, he decided, as he stampeded out the door.

The thin, hairy lab coat made a dive for Eddy and caught hold of his arm. His cat-scratched arm. That did not feel too great. Eddy shook him off and kept going. The thick lab coat grabbed his good arm. Well, if he wanted to come along so badly, Eddy guessed he could. And Eddy kept going.

Presently, a nurse coming down the hall was surprised to see Eddy going up the hall, with two doctors in tow.

"Where's Jack? Jack SuLong?" Eddy asked her.

"Get help!" the hairy doctor cried. "He's mad!"

The nurse turned and withdrew hastily.

Annoyed by that last comment regarding his sanity, Eddy grabbed the commentator and lifted his feet off the floor. Holding him helpless against the wall, he looked him square in the eye. "Mad, am I? Is that what you call it? Doctor, you haven't seen mad yet! I happen to want to see my wife and my friends, and you had better not stand in the way or you'll see downright grumpy!"

Setting the doctor down gently, Eddy started back up the hall. At the same instant, two male orderlies turned the corner and formed a human blockade. Ah, so now they wanted to play rugby. Eddy complied and kept going.

Presently, Maria, sitting in a waiting room, was surprised by a sudden commotion. It was caused by none other than her own dear husband: barefooted, bare-chested Eddy with a large retinue.

"Maria!" he exclaimed in relief, shaking off doctors and nurses like a dog shakes off water. He caught her up in his arms and kissed her good and long right there in front of them all.

"Maria—you okay?"

"I'm fine, Ed. At least, it's nothing that won't wear off." She took his face in her hands and kissed him again.

"Get your grimy hands off of me!" Eddy bristled.

The orderly let go of Eddy's elbow and stepped back a respectful distance.

Maria bit her lip and smiled. "How are you, darling?"

"Just fine," said Eddy. "I feel like I've been hit by a camel carrying a ton of bricks, but I'm fine. Have you heard anything about the others? Jack, is he going to—"

"I don't know. Jack and Carl are both in surgery now. And Camille has a fractured ankle."

"What? And we made her walk on it!" said Eddy.

"You couldn't know, Eddy. The x-ray barely caught it. You did your best. And anyway, we all made it back. We wouldn't have without you."

"Without Carl, you mean. And Jack. Jack's the real hero."

"Let's not talk about that now!" Maria begged, hugging him harder.

Eddy rested his cheek on her head, inhaling the comforting smell of her dirty, sweaty hair. He was in no hurry to leave, nor retire from the scene they were making in the middle of the busy waiting room. People could talk, people could stare, but this was his wife, and he loved her.

"Eddy," Maria said after several minutes. "Eddy, you really should go back to bed and rest."

Eddy did not even open his eye. "Maria, if that doctor is signing what he wants you to tell me, you can tell him to go jump in a lake. And make it a cold one!"

He felt her smile, and they stood there for several more minutes.

"Eddy, I hope you didn't hurt anyone."

"Now Maria, I was *very careful* with them!"

"But there's a man over here holding his eye: I think he'll have a good shiner."

"Oh, well he walked into that one," Eddy excused.

At length, he stood back and took a look at her, squinting slightly through his one eye. "Well, girl, I guess that will have to suffice for now." He turned to address the medical huddle. "I am now going to walk quietly back to my room with my wife. If any of you think you need either prevent or facilitate this process, step forward now and I'll imprint your face in that wall. If anyone wants to go another round, I'm going to ask you to sign a liability waiver. What, no takers? Okay then." He took his wife's hand. "Let's go, Maria."

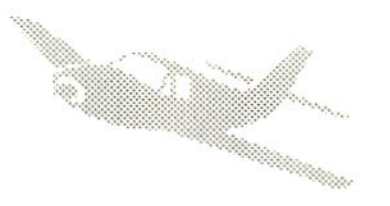

CHAPTER EIGHTEEN

SECRETS OF AN IVORY BOX

ONE WEEK LATER

Doctor Robert Martin sat in conference with Doctors Simone and Lucas, the two physicians who claimed responsibility for his son. He waited patiently through their evidence, their arguments, their charts, test results, x-ray films, statistics, opinions, second opinions, and finally, their diagnosis.

"Well?" said Doctor Lucas at last. "What do you think?"

"Well," said Doctor Martin, rising from his chair. "I see you have been very thorough in your research, gentlemen. My compliments."

The doctors beamed.

"Your diagnosis was stated very clearly, and though I am not a brain man myself, I can see from your charts that an injury to 'x' portion of the brain should produce 'y' as a result. Indeed, it is a very compelling argument you present." He paused to glance over a map of the human brain.

"However, you have neglected to take into account one thing."

The doctors leaned forward as one. "Yes?"

"The miraculous, created ability of the body to heal itself. Yes, I see that an injury to such a vulnerable area, and with such force as we can only imagine, would naturally produce these lasting negative effects. But I don't see that in my son. Yes, I'm told he was confused, amnesiac, and at certain times even dangerous. But I've also seen those symptoms in patients with moderate concussions."

He read off the notes the doctors had made. "'Lapses of memory.' Yes, as a boy Eddy experienced lapses of memory not infrequently. Chiefly in regard to breaking his mother's favorite vase or teapot, or the misplacement of the house keys. But he came around. 'Impaired judgment': well, that could just as easily refer to the both of you when you decided to tell me my son was a half-wit and doomed to stay that way."

Lucas and Simone began to look distinctly uncomfortable.

"And as for that last, 'sudden, erratic behavior,' I couldn't have described it better myself. Though always before I had thought in terms of boyish energy and youthful vigor. But yes, I would say that describes Edward to a tee.

"So you see, gentlemen, whereas you have convinced me that my son was gravely injured, you have not convinced me that he must stay that way. I have conversed with him at great length this week, testing his memory, calculation, and reasoning capabilities. Yes, there are loopholes, idiosyncrasies, if you will. But I believe the boy is on the mend. And he will mend best where he is most comfortable. So thank you, gentlemen, for your time and attention to my son: I am now going to take him home."

Doctor Martin gathered his hat, coat, and briefcase. Pausing at the door he said, "Never be afraid to throw out what the medical experts tell you *should be*, in favor of what *is*. And now, gentlemen, you know the secret of my success."

ꕥ ꕥ ꕥ

"Oh, it's you," Eddy remarked, pitching aside the book he had grabbed up and feigned reading. Maria turned back toward Eddy's bed, straightening the feather in her hat.

Dr. Martin looked from one to the other of them with a raised brow. "Yes, only me," he replied, waving a hand through the air in front of him. "Bit warm in here, isn't it?"

"I think it's cold," said Eddy, snatching at Maria's hand.

She jumped back. "Oh no you don't," she reprimanded. "You're a very naughty boy! Here I am, still telling you goodbye when I should have left an hour ago. I have half-a-dozen errands to run, and the housework yet to do, and if you're coming home today, there will need to be food—"

Eddy moaned. "There, Nursey, all that nonsense is making my head hurt."

"I'm afraid it will just have to hurt, then," she said severely, "because I have to get going."

"But maybe I'm not going home today," Eddy countered. "Maybe I'll never get home at all: maybe I'm a confirmed lunatic, and they're sending me straight to the bughouse, and then won't you be sorry for the way you're treating me?"

"That is easy enough to clear up." She turned to her father-in-law. "If you please, sir, what is the verdict on this scheming simpleton?"

"Edward Daniel Martin, you have been charged and found guilty of insanity, characterized by memory lapses, impaired judgment, and sudden, erratic behavior. However, the judge has determined that this is also perfectly normal for you, and has sentenced you to serve time at home in bed; sentence to be carried out immediately."

Maria clapped a hand over her mouth with a laugh.

"Perfectly normal!" Eddy exclaimed. "Thanks, Pop, I can see you were really sticking up for me in there!"

His father chuckled. "Are you ready to go home?"

"Am I? After a week of doctors and tests and 'let's have a look in that little ivory box of yours!'" Eddy rubbed his hands together in imitation of Dr. Simone and shuddered. "I'll say I'm ready!"

"Good. Then make yourself presentable," said Dr. Martin, producing a clean set of clothes for his son.

"I'll run along, now that I have half a chance," said Maria, blowing a kiss at Eddy.

He watched until the door closed behind her, then rubbed the heel of his hand over the side of his head. "Say, Dad, is there any hope for my eye?"

The doctor's lips compressed in that quick yet determined manner which Eddy recognized as the herald of bad news. "None," he answered. "Your optic nerve is quite dead."

Eddy drew a sharp breath, then shrugged. "I knew it was in trouble: couldn't see straight; started running into things. I guess that last bump on the prop really did it for me." He drew his shirt on and waited while his father buttoned it. "Well, that's the end of flying for me."

Dr. Martin was silent for several seconds. "It doesn't need to be, Eddy."

Eddy nodded. "But I think it is," he replied quietly.

"Maria won't mind that."

"No, she won't," Eddy agreed. "And somehow . . . somehow it doesn't bother me much, either." He drifted off, and then his voice returned, constricted and hoarse. "Dad? I'd like to see Jack and Carl before I go."

"Carl would be glad for a visit."

"But Jack? Maria's tried three times this week, and he wouldn't see her. What's wrong, Dad? Something I did?"

"Jack is paralyzed," said Dr. Martin.

Eddy blinked and sat back deeper in the bed, the air sucked from his lungs. "But . . . but, how? The lead wasn't—didn't touch the spine. It was something I did, then. Or something I didn't do."

"No, Eddy, you did well. Under the circumstances, you did what you could. Unfortunately, a bone fragment severed the spinal cord. Jack is paraplegic. That's why he would not see Maria, why he hasn't had visitors. He's grieving, and needs to come to grips with his loss before he can share it."

Eddy moaned. "Then it was me. If I'd extracted the bone before moving him . . ."

Dr. Martin pulled up a chair and sat down very slowly. "If you had tried that, you'd have killed him with shock. You did all you could, Eddy."

"But it wasn't good enough!" Eddy cried, dropping his head into his hands.

Dr. Martin groaned deep inside. "Every doctor experiences feelings of inadequacy at one time or another. I was with your mother when she died, Eddy: right there with her, but all I could do was hold her hand and cry." The old doctor's eyes were glistening at the memory. "There are two things doctors have never done and will never do in the future: create life, and stop death. Oh yes, the One who has power over both may use our hands to stave off death for a season. But we can never thwart it indefinitely." He stood and squeezed Eddy's shoulder. "I'm proud of what you did," he said quietly. "I'm proud of you, son. Now, come on. Put a brave face on it, and I'll see you get ten minutes with both Jack and Carl before we go."

හ ଔ හ

Eddy tried to brace up for Jack, but one sight of his friend, immobilized in plaster, and his resolve crumbled. He stopped just inside the door.

"Hi, Jack."

"What do you think I am?" Jack bellowed from the bed. "A highwayman? Hijack, my eye! Get in here!"

Blinking and swallowing hard, Eddy moved forward on lead feet.

"Well, take a look at your work: aren't I done up pretty?" He knocked his knuckles on the cast. "Plenty of room for signatures on this beauty."

Eddy winced. "Jack, I—"

"Everyone says you did a fine job."

"Jack, I'm so—"

"Maybe you'd like to check my progress? Take a few x-ray films, while you're at it."

Eddy threw himself into a chair with a great sob. "I'm sorry, Jack! So sorry!"

"Oh, shut up," Jack growled. He looked at Eddy. "Or tell me to! Come on, Ed. I'm not angry with you."

Eddy lifted his head, another apology on his lips, but Jack cut in.

"I *was* angry at first," he admitted. "Oh, not for being . . . paralyzed." He said the word slowly, as though testing it for the first time. "Wasn't that. Just—I *told* you not to bother; *told* you to let me be. It was too much for you, Eddy. You'd have gotten over me a lot sooner if you'd just left me there. Now . . . Well, neither of us got what we wanted."

For the first time Eddy could remember, he saw water shining in Jack's eyes.

"I'm tired of it, Eddy. Tired of being lonely. Tired of waking in the morning and wondering why I took the trouble. I miss Pearl; my boys! I—"

Suddenly realizing he had allowed himself to get more emotional than he had meant, Jack eyed Eddy with the bashfulness of a small child.

"Oh, you probably didn't know . . ."

"Carl told me," Eddy said gently.

"Carl. Yeah, I guess he heard, all right. I've tried to keep it quiet all these years because I hated to be pitied; hated it when a room went silent whenever I entered. I thought the pain would go away. But it never did."

Eddy drew a deep breath. "That's because you've bottled it up. You're healed on the outside, but inside you're all full of infection. You'll have to open it up and clean it out—it won't be pretty and it won't be pleasant; but that's the only way you'll ever heal."

Jack was silent a long time, his eyes squeezed resentfully at the moisture building at their corners. Then at last, mouth twisting as he summoned the levity for a reply, "Taking up cardiology now, are you? Why don't you have a talk with that fool Linder and let him know there's no disgrace in cutting in on a corpse?"

"I plan to," said Eddy. "But the rumor is he's already made a move in that direction."

"Has he? About time. How is the old bird? How's Carl? I haven't heard a thing. Camille? How's Maria? Did you all get out okay?"

"Yes, Jack. Thanks to you. Camille's home with a fractured ankle, and Carl's a bit bunged up: rib punctured a lung during that last little marathon he ran. But we made it; thanks to you and—"

The door swung open, saving Eddy from a second show of tears. Doctor Martin poked his head in. "Ten minutes, Eddy."

"You shipping out?" asked Jack.

"I'm shipping home. Just after I stop in to see Carl."

"Well, say hi for me."

"Sure, Jack." Eddy was almost through the door.

"Oh hey, Eddy?"

"What is it?"

"My address isn't going to change for a while: come back when you can?"

"Sure, Jack," Eddy assented. "Glad to."

ꟹ ꟹ ꟹ

Eddy burst into Carl's room. "Hi Carl! Good to see you, buddy!"

Carl smiled and lifted two fingers in response to Eddy's greeting.

"Hey, you don't look too bad," Eddy commented.

"Oh? I don't feel too good," Carl rasped. "How're you?"

"Got my discharge papers today. Pops busted me out."

"Wish he'd do that for me sometime."

"Sure; when do you want it?"

"Maybe not for a while yet," Carl conceded. He paused and put forth a concentrated effort to draw a long breath. "How's Jack?"

Eddy sat down, clasping both hands in his lap. "Not too good, Carl. He's . . . He won't walk ever again. He's paralyzed."

Carl's eyes opened wider for a second. It seemed an eternity before he spoke. "Poor Jack. How's he taking it?"

"Pretty well, all things considered. He sends his greetings." Eddy paused. "He mentioned Pearl."

Carl looked hard at Eddy. "Really? That has to be a first since—"

Eddy nodded again. "Since the boat headed stateside and the ravings of a fevered invalid. And coming on six years since it happened. That's a long time to be carrying it around inside."

"Stubborn old goat! What's he planning to do now?"

"We didn't go into that," Eddy admitted. He banged the back of one hand into the palm of the other. "But I'm just sure Mr. Jensen would find something for him—"

"Nah!" Carl interrupted. "He wouldn't want that. Wouldn't want to be around planes, if he couldn't fly 'em. I know I sure wouldn't."

Eddy was silent a moment. "Yeah. Me either, Carl."

Carl's eyebrows went up. "Your eye?"

Eddy nodded. Then shrugged. "Partly. And partly . . . I'm thinking I'll go back to school: finish that degree."

"Well, well, well. So it'll be Doc Martingale, after all. Congratulations."

"It seems a bit early for that," Eddy started with a grin. "But sources tell me you might be in the way of needing them."

Carl tried to smile just as a spasm of pain hit his lung, and the effect was a bit sour. "Haven't asked yet," he admitted. The spasm passed and he drew a little breath. "Though she's reminded me twice already. I'm letting the anticipation build a little: I want to do it up proper this time. Lying flat on my back doesn't seem quite—"

Eddy laughed and patted Carl on the shoulder. "Don't worry—if you get cold feet and try to back out, your friends will be right behind you."

Carl changed the subject with some of his old alacrity. "Say, Eddy? Got who?"

Eddy frowned. "Huh?"

"You said I got him: you mean . . . ?"

"Atgood." The single word came out as rough as tree bark. "I found him about fifty yards below the cabin in a pile of brush. Right- or left-handed, you've still got it, buddy!"

Carl raised one side of his mouth. "That doesn't help Jack any," he answered ruefully. He looked up suddenly. "Did they ever take care of Westman?"

A nod. "He's had a decent burial."

"Poor kid. And the jacket?"

"I'd forgotten about that," said Eddy. "I guess Inspector Rigby will know what to do with it."

"Inspector? Then they're investigating. Smuggling?"

Eddy inclined his head. "Likely, I'd say. But of course, *they're* not saying."

"And we were played," Carl muttered.

"You know, there's bound to be some questions later on," Eddy warned. "We may even be called as witnesses."

Carl's nose wrinkled up and, Eddy thought, his tongue was a quarter-inch from poking between his front teeth. "Well, I don't care for questions," he said. "If they want me, they'll have to find me."

"Oh? And where will you be so well concealed?"

Carl yawned. "I was thinking Switzerland."

Eddy blinked twice. "Switzerland? I thought you and—"

"I don't plan to go alone, you understand." Carl looked past Eddy at the far wall. "But still, if it comes to that," he said slowly, "I have some old friends there: thought I'd like to renew their acquaintance."

"You mean Dr. Emminger?"

"Right. Saved my life, he did; took care of me after I got out of Germany. I was such a goner. But I didn't have time to thank him then. So I figure I'll look him up and settle the score."

"Sounds like a good idea to me," Eddy nodded as his father stepped in to remind him of the time. "But whatever you do," he advised, "don't go alone."

CHAPTER NINETEEN

A TELLING SOUVENIR

APRIL, 1948

Eggs spattered as they hit the hot pan. Maria paused, another white, speckled oval between her fingertips.

"Three or four eggs, Eddy?"

No answer came, and she turned to see him in his chair at the table, bent over, resting his forehead on a book. His tea was untouched beside him. This was his favorite study position of late; between schooling days and working nights, he was exhausted. Maria continually reminded him that he could not absorb information from a textbook simply by sleeping with his head pillowed on it. Eddy, it seemed, was bound and determined to prove her wrong. And so far, his marks sided with him. Maria just wondered how long he could keep it up.

"Eddy, dear." She came behind him and kneaded his shoulders. "If you're so tired, why don't you go back to bed?"

His head popped up and he stared bleary eyed at the book in front of him. "No time. Have to study," he said, yawning. "Big exam Monday." His hand felt for the eyeglasses that lay askew on the table, and he wrestled them onto his face.

"You've passed your other exams with flying colors."

"I studied better for them."

"Well, this kind of study won't help anything!" Maria admonished. She flipped the book closed amid his protests and shoved it aside. "Oh! Now I'm burning the eggs."

He laughed as she hurried back to the stove to save breakfast.

"Not as bad as they could be," she apologized, serving him eggs with whites glazed a dark brown. Joining him at the table, she sifted through a small stack of envelopes. "Did you happen to look at yesterday's mail?"

Eddy sloshed tepid tea after orange marmalade on toast. "Didn't have time. Besides, what do we get but bills and solicitations?"

"Oh, not much," Maria agreed, drawing a small envelope from the rest and dancing it on the table in front of him. "But this one has an interesting postmark."

Eddy squinted. "Is that Hawaii? Jack!" He snatched the letter and slit it with his butter knife, shaking out a handwritten note and a photograph. Maria leaned close and they studied the picture together. Sitting below a shop sign reading *SuLong's Souvenirs,* a half-startled Jack looked up at them, eyebrows raised, mouth partly open. In his hands, one could see a block of wood beginning to take the form of an aircraft under the inducement of his knife. But the part that made Eddy chuckle and Maria smile was the little, dark head that bent close to Jack's work; the little hand resting on the arm of Jack's wheelchair, the other hand that pointed a finger as if directing the process.

"Well," Eddy grinned. "That's Jack. Looks like he's found his niche. He'll be okay." He sniffed and took a long drink of his tea as Maria unfolded the note.

Dear Eddy and Maria,

Here's the update on me, as you can see. Nephew Stu is ever the slave driver.

Sorry to skip out before our Swiss expedition returned. Say all the proper things for me when they do.

So long,

SuLong

PS Give me ten minutes' notice before you come, and I'll order sunshine with a side of fresh pineapple just for you.

—J.

Eddy grinned. "I guess he hasn't lost his sense of humor."

"He looks happy," said Maria.

"Or close to it."

"Hawaii's done wonders for him, don't you think?"

Eddy grunted his agreement and picked up the photo again, only vaguely aware that he was hearing words like "sunshine," "beach," and "palm trees" in the background. Jack was happy. For the moment, that was all that mattered.

A sudden change in the tone of Maria's voice cut into his thoughts. "We should go, darling."

"Oh yes, definitely," Eddy agreed. "Maybe next year."

"Next year seems a little late."

Eddy chuckled and shook his head. "I don't see how we can manage a vacation any earlier."

"A vaca—" Maria beamed. "All right, I'll take it; but what I said was, we should be leaving for the courthouse." She gathered Eddy's empty dishes and turned toward the sink.

"The courthouse?" Eddy twisted in his chair. "Now, if I'm not mistaken, my dear, I married you some years ago."

"Yes, dear. In a church."

"Good and proper," said Eddy as Maria slipped back to the bedroom to gather her things. "Have I incurred excessive library fees?"

"No," Maria called from the hall.

"Parking tickets?"

She reappeared, buttoning a navy-blue cape around her shoulders. "None that I'm aware of."

"Then what?"

"The hearing. Put on your shoes, dear. They're under the table, just at your feet."

Thoughtful, Eddy shoved his feet one by one into the shoes and laced them. "Hearing? I hadn't worried so much about my hearing. It's my memory concerns me more."

In answer, Maria laid two fingers on Eddy's wrist and consulted her watch.

"That bad, am I?" Eddy asked.

"Afraid so," said Maria, pulling on her gloves. "In fact, if we are not out of this house in precisely thirty seconds, we will be well and truly late." She settled his hat onto his head.

Eddy adjusted his hat so it sat just off center. "Funny. I have this feeling of being rushed out of the house, whither, I know not."

"To the hearing!" Maria exclaimed. "Benjamin T. Ferguson, mechanic for the late Milford Smith."

"Oh! That's today?"

"That's right now."

"I told you not to let me forget."

Maria smiled as she helped him catch the sleeve of his jacket and slip his arm into it. "I reminded you first thing this morning."

"Somehow," Eddy sighed, "that's not the same thing."

Their arrival in the courtroom was celebrated with a laconic nod from Harry Jensen. "Well, you're out early. Didn't expect you for another half hour."

"I make it a point to be almost on time once every third try," Eddy returned as he seated Maria in one of the overly straight chairs and took his beside Harry. "Did we miss anything?"

"Sure," Harry griped, rubbing a hand over his chin. "Waiting. They've been in their back room, wrangling a way out of this mess. Plea bargain. Turns out Ferguson doesn't want to face the music. Not that I blame him: this could look an awful lot like murder conspiracy to a jury." He nodded across the aisle, at a woman sitting alone, conspicuous in her choice of black garments and the contrasting limp white handkerchief, which she applied to her eyes from time to time.

"The little wife," Harry explained.

Eddy wished he had not known. His fingers itched for his own handkerchief, a small gesture to show he bore no ill will. A glance over his right shoulder to see who else might be there revealed a couple of newsmen: wishful of excitement, despairing of its occurrence, their cameras dangling over their knees. A young boy with his mother, notebook in hand, doodled on the page that should have been filling up with notes for his school assignment. Two policemen lounged at the back; and the inspector, irritated by delay, paced and frowned and shoved hands deep in his pockets.

Directly behind him, Eddy heard a familiar voice, low and conspiratorial, and a slight bit giddy. He turned his head to the left. Bad eye. He twisted to the right. A newspaper headline sprouted, spreading itself across two chair breadths. Eddy wrenched around in his seat and swiped the paper down with an exclamation.

"Carl!"

Eddy did a double take, for there, snuggled close to Carl's side, was a Camille completely unlike any he had ever seen. The guilty party, seated beside his still-blushing bride, pulled the paper from Eddy's grasp.

"Look here, no peeking! When do the lights go down in this lousy theater, anyway?"

"Carl, you sneaky rascal! We didn't expect you back until tomorrow. You just couldn't stay away from us, could you?"

"Not another minute!" Carl laughed, slapping Eddy on the back.

"Camille, you're—" Eddy stopped, ill-prepared to explain a transformation wrought by upswept hair and a tailored suit of light blue. "You look great," he finished, then grinned and jerked a thumb at Carl. "Why'd you bring him back, Camille? You coulda got rid of him for good."

"Oh, I rather doubt that!" Carl objected loudly.

Camille reached a hand to pat Carl's face. "I don't know," she replied. "I guess I've gotten used to having him around. Besides, what would Uncle Harry do without him?"

Harry's answering guffaw drew all eyes present in their direction. "I'd get ahead in the world, that's what I'd do.

Question is, what am I going to do without my little Camille?"

"You're not losing me, Uncle, you're gaining a—"

"Yeah," he cut in. "I've seen the end of that line before." He shook his head. "I'm sure gonna miss you."

"Well, you all are scads of fun," said Carl, "but just so happens I'm a wee bit starved. What do you think, darling, a nice big steak dinner at Jimmy's?"

"Whatever you like," she smiled.

Eddy laughed. "You've got your menu plan all cockeyed! When'd you get in?"

"Late last night."

"Or early this morning," Camille amended, her fingers toying with a brooch on her lapel.

Maria reached her hand out to examine it. "That's a clever pin, Camille. What is it?"

Camille blushed. "I don't know," she admitted. "Carl was so silly: he kept wanting to buy things. I had to make him stop."

"Oh, but she made everything look so good!" Carl exclaimed. "I had every clothier in Switzerland wanting to steal her from me to model their line."

Pink turned to rose, and Camille lowered her eyes.

"See what it does to her," Carl confided to Eddy. "Becoming-er and becoming-er. Now that gives me a good idea," he added, and with a flourish of his newspaper, delivered something slightly more elaborate than a quick peck on the cheek.

"Say, speaking of trinkets," Carl went on, relaxing his barricade, "Whatever became of those rocks we found?"

"They were traced to Europe," said Harry. "Owned by a Jewish merchant, one Abram Horovitz, or something like it. He disappeared into a camp, and his property was all confiscated."

"And how they came to be in a jacket liner on the body of a young pilot in the Rockies—" Eddy began.

"Two words," Harry cut in. "Milford Smith. He had fingers in everything. The real riddle is what happened to the other airplane. A man doesn't usually go to much trouble to kill his grandson and lose a pocketful of diamonds, unless he's tetched. That's not to say Milford wasn't," Harry added. "But sabotaging his own airplane about takes the cake. I'm convinced he meant that trick with the oilpan for someone else—someone who got off scot-free."

Carl snorted. "How's that for being in the wrong place at the wrong time?"

"Well, if it's any comfort," said Eddy, waxing poetic, "Though we perish in the teeth, yet there is no animosity in the jaws."

Carl stood and placed his hand over his heart. "I'm deeply moved," he said. "Either that, or it was my stomach. I'm going with the latter. Camille, I grow weak. If it's Jimmy's, then let us hasten thither—"

Eddy laughed. "You grow weak, do you? My boy, you've plain been growing! Looks like Switzerland hasn't been too hard on you. Are you going to start wearing man-sized trousers soon?"

"Maybe." Carl patted his beltline, then patted Eddy on the head. "Are you going to start wearing long trousers soon?"

"Well, let's get this show moving," Harry interrupted. "You hungry, Eddy? I'm buying."

Eddy glanced at Maria. "Not that I feel unfed," he began.

"We're coming," Maria confirmed.

They passed through the double doors, their high humor unfitting for the somber halls of justice. In his distraction, Carl jostled shoulders with a man moving the opposite direction.

"Pardon me." The words were out of his mouth before he looked around to see the man who had been sharing elbow space with him. The other party did not look back. Yet something struck Carl as vaguely familiar in the folds of skin on the back of his neck. He stared.

"That suit you, Carl?"

"Huh?"

Eddy laughed. "For as starved as you are, you're sure distracted. I said—"

Carl glanced over his shoulder. That man. Wearing a black suit. Escorted by an officer of the law. They entered a courtroom.

". . . so if that's okay with you, Carl. Carl?"

"Yeah. Swell. I—uh—forgot something. I'll be right . . ." He swung away.

"Carl? Carl!" Camille started after him, then stopped. He had not even looked back. She turned to Eddy, her eyes filling.

"Has he been like this?" Eddy asked.

Camille shook her head. "No. I don't understand."

Eddy patted her hand. "You go ahead. I'll see what's going on."

ꟸ ꟸ ꟸ

Archibald Black, pleading "not guilty" to charges of resisting arrest, assaulting a police officer, falsifying documents, etcetera. Carl sighed. He was not acquainted with any Archibald Black. And this trial was likely to be long and boring.

But what about that head? The skin, red with lines even when the wrinkles pulled straight. Who did he know that was bald and rather flat on top? A third-grade schoolmaster? An orderly from the children's hospital? Milkman? None of them fit the bill. But he had to know.

The defendant turned slightly to counsel with his lawyer, giving Carl a three-quarter view from behind. The tip of that nose—sort of bulbous and red. Vaguely familiar. Or was he mistaken?

"What's up, Carl?" Eddy touched his shoulder. "You get yourself a wild hair?"

Carl jabbed Eddy in the ribs with his elbow and warned him to be quiet.

"Hey, you know you've kind of startled the wife—"

Carl stepped on Eddy's toes in passing him in the narrow chair row. He moved slowly up the middle aisle. Moved? Stalked.

Eddy started to follow. "Hey, Carl—"

The judge glared and pointed his gavel. "See here you, what do you think—"

Carl reached his objective. He tapped the defendant on the shoulder. The man turned. Carl sucked in his breath—and gave him a mouthful of fist just as hard as he could.

Order devolved to chaos. The man fell from his chair. The press surged forward, flash bulbs popping. People made a general din. The judge pounded. Carl did not notice. He was in a tunnel, alone with this man, and he was going to kill him.

"Carl! Carl, get ahold of yourself!"

"Let go of me, Eddy, or I'll hit you, too!"

Eddy forced Carl's arm up behind his back; a bailiff took the other side. Both struggled against Carl while the accused wiped blood from his lip and struggled to his feet.

"I will have order!" the judge bellowed. "Order in my court!"

The bailiff seated Carl and cuffed one arm to the chair.

"Young man," the judge snarled, "I find you in contempt of court!"

Eddy stepped forward. "Please, Your Honor, he didn't mean anything—"

"Sit!" the judge demanded.

Eddy did so.

Carl stared silently at the man for several seconds, realizing the consequences of what he had done would be severe. But he was past the point of no return already.

"Well?" the judge asked impatiently. "Have you anything to say for yourself?"

Carl drew a deep breath and looked up. "Yes, I have, Your Honor. Plenty." He stood, picking up the chair in his cuffed hand, and strode across the room to the defense table. Using the chair as an extension of his arm, he gestured vigorously. "Your Honor, this man fills your courtroom with contempt—and not because of the piddly crime for which he sits before you today. Oh no! His crimes are against all humanity. This man, this 'Archibald Black,' as he calls himself, is none other than Gustaf Hersch—"

Across the aisle, the defendant exploded from his seat. From the back of the room, a bullet exploded from its barrel. It struck Carl in the shoulder. Another bullet cut the air over his head. Carl saw the shooter disappear through the courtroom doors as he dropped to the floor. More shots followed outside.

"Carl! You get yourself into more trouble . . ." Eddy bent over Carl and checked the wound.

Carl coughed and sputtered.

"Eh, you'll be okay—you'll be fine." Eddy pressed his thumb into a place that burned hot and bright. "Just lie still, we'll get you fixed up."

"Herschner," Carl whispered. "Gustaf Herschner."

"I hear you, kid."

The judge knelt in his robes beside Carl. "Young man, we have an ambulance on the way. In the meantime, if you can talk, I'm all ears. If they wanted to stop you that badly, it must be important."

"Gustaf Herschner," Carl repeated.

"Archibald Black is Gustaf Herschner," the judge nodded. "Who is Gustaf Herschner?"

Words were slow and faltering. "Nazi . . . Gestapo . . . war crimes in . . . camp . . ."

The judge leaned close to hear. "How do you know all this, son?"

Carl reached a hand toward his throat. Eddy thought he was choking at first, but then it became clear. Eddy unbuttoned Carl's second and third shirt button, opening it to expose his chest. A tattoo: #839185.

The judge drew in his breath and let it out slowly. "I see," he said at last. "They'll want you as a witness at his trial, son."

"I'll be there," said Carl.

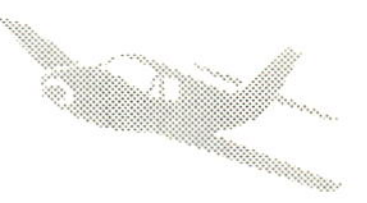

EPILOGUE

Gustaf Herschner of the Nazi Gestapo, alias Archibald Black, was tried before a military court and found guilty. Unlike many of his victims, his death was quick and relatively painless. His accomplice, Ronald Schultz, was gunned down in the courthouse hallway after his attempted assassination of Carl Linder.

Carl and Camille enjoyed many years together, sharing the joys and trials of raising a large family. Carl continued to work at Jensen Manufacturing Company, which soon became Jensen and Linder Manufacturing Company, and eventually Linder and Sons. George Tumball became a valuable employee.

Despite many frailties, Camille lived to the age of sixty-two, when she was taken suddenly by a heart attack. Carl never remarried. Some years later, he returned to Germany to visit the camp where he was incarcerated. Though asked numerous times to speak publicly of his experiences, he never did. He shared on a small scale with those who sought him out, but feared too much publicity would make a hero of him.

For the remainder of his years, Carl returned to Switzerland, his chosen home. It was one morning after a brisk hike, which was his daily habit, that he was found asleep in his bed, never to be roused. He was seventy-five.

Jack lived many years with his extended family in Hawaii. A constant at the souvenir shoppe, and a favorite among the boys who visited, he filled the role of father to many. But it was during his sixth decade that he reclaimed the title of husband, when he met, married, and grew old with Lolita, a war widow with three grown sons.

Eddy and Maria experienced great heartache with the loss of their first child at birth. A second stillbirth, coupled with Maria's impatience to raise a family, prompted them to adopt two girls from England—sisters who had lost their parents during the London bombing. They were in the process of adopting another when Eddy Junior arrived on the scene. The only Martin blood of that generation to reach adulthood, his father lost no opportunity to impart the skills of hunting, fishing, and tracking, while Maria made certain each of the girls could start a fire and keep camp.

Like Dr. Robert Martin before him, Eddy became a successful physician, specializing in family medicine. His genuine compassion for the individual and gentle bedside manner set him in good stead with his patients. It was with great sorrow that the small community in Colorado learned of the loss of their doctor and his beloved wife in an automobile crash in 1988. Eddy had been practicing for thirty-six years, and had often said that death would be his retirement.

This is not the end of the story. The descendants of the characters mentioned herein continued in the line of their fathers; and like their sires, were faced with choices: decisions every day, for good or for evil. Some chose the noble way, holding to a high standard of honor and self-sacrifice. Others took the low road, sinking into the depths of dishonesty and despair. But all, in one respect, were alike: all were faced with a choice. And all were held accountable for their choice. Even as we are today.

> *"And if it seem evil unto you to serve the LORD, choose you this day whom ye will serve; . . . but as for me and my house, we will serve the LORD."*
>
> *—Joshua 24:15 KJV*

Printed in the United States
by Baker & Taylor Publisher Services